For a moment she couldn't move

Emile was sitting in his armchair, eyes closed. His lean fingers curled around an empty brandy glass. April's heart contracted at the sight of him.

His hair looked grayer, his mouth was set, stamped with the cruelty of what life had presented to him — a cruelty she had unwittingly added to. He looked utterly, utterly desolate.

"What is it, Finn?" he asked. "Why are you hovering?"

"I'm hovering because I don't quite know whether I'm welcome, " she said softly.

For a moment he was completely without control. April saw the pain, the pleasure and confusion on his face as he jerked upright in his chair. "April! What — why are you here?" Then in a voice not at all reminiscent of the velvety softness she remembered, he demanded, "What the hell do you want?"

The Melting Heart

Claudia Jameson

Harlequin Books

TORONTO • NEW YORK • LONDON
AMSTERDAM • PARIS • SYDNEY • HAMBURG
STOCKHOLM • ATHENS • TOKYO • MILAN

Original hardcover edition published in 1983
by Mills & Boon Limited

ISBN 0-373-02565-3

Harlequin Romance first edition August 1983

Printed in the U.S.A.

CHAPTER ONE

'JUST look at this weather! Who'd have expected this, in the middle of March?' April Baxter joined her brother at the breakfast table, her eyes travelling towards the windows and the heavy fall of snow which had gathered during the night.

'Good morning, April.' Alan handed her a cup of tea and moved the milk jug and cornflakes over to her side of the table. 'This is England, my dear. We do get snow in March, you know. But you'd better allow yourself extra time for getting to Buckinghamshire. There's a wind getting up, and there might be snowdrifts out in the country. What time's your interview?'

'Three o'clock.' She'd already told him that. 'Alan, about our discussion last night—won't you reconsider?'

'No.' He said it firmly, very firmly. Then he smiled as if to apologise. 'It's very sweet of you, Sis, but you've already done enough for your family in the past. I'm not going to rob you of your youth by letting you act as unpaid housekeeper and surrogate mother to my two kids.'

April's spoonful of cornflakes stopped in mid-air. She put it down again and laughed at her brother's choice of words. 'Rob me of my youth? I'm nearly twenty-four already, and I don't exactly live the high life! You wouldn't be robbing me of anything! It'd just be a case of swapping one job for another——'

'Have you got directions for getting to this place in

Bucks?' Alan cut in. She knew then that the subject was closed. He would not allow her to move in with him, to look after his house and two children, even though Robert and Sally were her nephew and niece, and they desperately needed someone to look after them. Well, not just to look after them, but to *care* for them. All of them.

April picked up her tea and eyed her brother over the rim of her cup. Just six months short of forty, he had a rapidly receding hairline and there were lines of strain around his eyes and mouth. Despite that, he was still a good-looking man, far better looking than April. She had a similar shade of dark blond hair, but with her pale skin and the faint scattering of freckles she detested, on her it could only be described as mousey. Their eyes were similar, too, except that Alan's were somehow greener, and larger, whereas April regarded hers as nondescript.

Alan was a lonely man, although he denied it. He had recovered from the shock of his wife's death quite well, thanks to the children and their tremendous need of him. But he worked too hard, coping with the demands of his office during the day and those of a nine- and ten-year-old during the evening. The strain was beginning to show, and April worried about him.

April's greatest wish was that her brother would meet someone and remarry. Someone—someone even half as good and kind as his first wife, who would make them into a complete family again. There wasn't much chance of that happening, though. Alan's social life was non-existent, and despite the fact that April usually spent every other weekend at the house, a readily available babysitter, he never took the opportunity of going out.

'Have you switched me off, or something?' He leaned over and gave her a gentle nudge. 'I was asking if you had directions for getting to your interview. Only, I can get out my road map and show you——'

'That's okay.' She smiled, fishing in her handbag for the paper on which she'd written the instructions given to her by her agency the previous day. The directions for finding the place in Buckinghamshire had been very explicit, although the details about her prospective employer, and the job itself, had not.

The phone call from the agency had come at five past five the previous day, Friday. Five o'clock was the agency's closing time, and Phyllis, the manageress, had been apologetic, explaining that she was in a hurry, had to dash off and catch a train as she was going away for the weekend. So she hadn't given April much detail about the assignment. She'd asked her to report to a Mr Finn, at a private house in Bucks. She'd said only that Mr Finn was a writer, that he needed a secretary very urgently but would wish to interview April before deciding whether to take her on.

April's current assignment had finished at noon that day, and she had actually been toying with the idea of taking a week off. But this was an emergency, Phyllis said, so she had agreed to see Mr Finn, had put some suitable clothing in the weekend case she was taking to Surrey, and had every intention of returning to her brother's house after her interview.

Handing back the slip of paper, Alan nodded. 'You'd better allow yourself about two and a half hours from here. Make it three,' he added, his eyes wandering to the windows and the drifts of snow that were piling up on the ledges. 'Isn't it rather unusual, being interviewed on a Saturday?'

'It's unusual that I should be interviewed at all! Normally we just get assigned to people, and that's that. The agency's name is recommendation enough!' April was mildly indignant. It had been a long, long time since she had actually been interviewed for a job. She wasn't an ordinary temp, she was a shorthand writer of the highest calibre, working for an exclusive London agency who handled only a few score people, all of whom were skilled in writing shorthand at a minimum of 140 words per minute. They were the tops in their profession, men and women alike, and probably the best typists in the country.

Before joining the Morrison Agency, April had spent two years as a shorthand writer in the law courts. Then she had had an eight-month absence from working life while she nursed her dying father. She had been diligent about keeping up her speed by taking down the news from radio and television, and had joined Morrison's after her father's death, when the family home had been sold and she had bought her own flat in Paddington.

Normally her assignments lasted anywhere between one day and one month. She had attended meetings and conferences of every size and nature, had frequently been required to travel out of London, and had in fact once before worked for a writer. What a boring assignment that had been! Fortunately, she had only been filling in for someone else, and the job had lasted just ten days. She had been working for a very old lady who had been writing a book about bee-keeping!

'If you get this job——'

'Which I will!' April put in. 'Interviews work two

ways, you know. I might decide not to take it when it's offered!'

Alan smiled at her abundance of confidence, especially as it was perfectly justified. 'If you are offered the assignment, and you take it, won't it be a drag commuting from London to Bucks every day? Driving there in the rush hour? I'd hate it.'

'Not at all. Besides, I'm paid for my travelling time, so it won't cost me anything. Have you forgotten the days when you used to travel from our parents' home, from the southernmost part of Kent to the City every day?'

He had been learning his profession then, and April had been just a little girl. Every evening he would come home, eat, then vanish into his room for hours on end, studying. Now, he worked locally as a solicitor. He was a partner in a small but busy practice in Guildford, Surrey.

Moving from Kent to Surrey was something Alan had done when he married Liz. He was still living in the same house, working in the same practice. April had suggested it might be better, for him and the children, to move to another house, perhaps on the other side of town, where the memories of Liz would not be there to remind them daily of their loss. But he had refused, insisting that it was good to keep memories alive, to stay in the house where they had all been so happy once.

'Where are the children?' she asked then, noticing how thickly the snow was coming down. 'In the back garden, I'll bet.'

'Where else? They're building a snowman.'

'They'll get soaked,' she fussed. 'Have they eaten?'

'Just cereal. I was about to make us bacon and eggs, actually. Do you fancy some?'

April looked heavenward and laughed. 'I'll do it. You stay there with your newspaper!'

For all his practicality, his ability to shop well, spend time with his children and keep up with the demands of his work, cooking was something Alan was incapable of. He even made a mess of boiling an egg. He wasn't too hot on housework, either. That was strange, really, when by nature he was a home-bird and in so many other ways very efficient and down-to-earth.

April sighed, reaching into the refrigerator and noticing that it badly needed defrosting. Perhaps Alan considered it more important to spend all his free time with his children. It was certainly obvious that since his daily woman had moved up north three weeks ago, his house had been sadly neglected.

Still, she had at least convinced her brother that he needed a full-time housekeeper. Last night they had had a long discussion—which had almost resulted in a row. April was so concerned for her niece and nephew, and for Alan, that she had offered to give up her own work and live with them, to look after them. It wasn't the first time she'd mentioned this idea, but they had never discussed it thoroughly before. Alan wouldn't hear of it. He said there was no way he would allow April to give up her career, move into a quiet little village and become a maiden aunt who had no life of her own.

There was no use arguing with him; Alan was as stubborn as the day was long. But he had admitted he needed someone full-time, and had agreed to advertise for a housekeeper. So April had made some progress, at least.

From the kitchen window she kept an eye on Sally and Robert, and the snowman's progress, as she cooked the breakfast, taking stock of her life in a rather abstract way.

Her work as a shorthand writer was enjoyable. It was certainly immensely varied and rarely boring, but she had reached the stage where nothing was new to her. After meeting all sorts of people, in all sorts of businesses and professions, she was no longer excited or challenged by her assignments.

Her days in the world of commerce were sometimes a little too hectic, too exhausting, her evenings as an unattractive bachelor girl often very empty. She honestly believed she would have been perfectly content to sell her flat, move in with her brother and be a substitute mother to his children, if only until they left school. She had reached the stage where she would welcome a slower pace of life and the company of her family in the evenings.

Marriage was something she did not think about. There was little point. While she was by no means starry-eyed, April knew that it would have to be an exceptional man who could persuade her to make a lifelong commitment. What she would want in a husband would be very hard to find. Having accepted that fact, April was also realistic; with her plain looks and a figure which had grown somewhat chubby of late, even ordinary men were not exactly queueing up to take her out!

Still, she was reasonably content. She was very well paid, expensively dressed, owned her own flat and car, and was totally self-sufficient, even if life in London did get rather lonely at times.

At twelve o'clock she left Alan's house for Buckinghamshire, certain she was leaving far too early, even allowing for the bad weather.

'I'll see you later this evening,' she told the children as they were seeing her off.

'Don't make that a promise,' warned Alan. 'This snow's being whipped up into a blizzard. If you decide to go straight home afterwards, we'll understand.'

'Don't fuss,' she told him. 'I'll be back. I've planned a big Sunday roast for us tomorrow. See you later.'

'Okay, good luck with the interview.'

April shrugged carelessly. 'It's just a job. I shall tell this Mr Finn he won't find a better secretary than I, and if he doesn't like the look of me, then it's his loss. I'll be able to take my pick of a dozen other assignments on Monday morning. I'll tell him all that!'

For a moment Alan looked aghast. Then he laughed heartily, 'Liar, you'll say nothing of the kind!'

April walked towards the garage, her laughter tinkling on the cold, crisp air, the snow crunching beneath her boots. Gosh, it was cold!

Her car started without any trouble, thanks to the fact that it had been sheltered in Alan's double garage. By the time she reached the motorway, the heater in the little Triumph was working full belt and she relaxed as the warmth filled the car. She was sensibly though smartly dressed in brown leather boots and a sheepskin coat. The first skirt she had tried on was too tight, now, around the waist, and she had only bought it just before Christmas, so she had settled for a camel-coloured wrapover skirt that had an adjustable fastening. With that and a matching lambswool sweater set off with a simple gold chain necklace, she looked every inch the smart, efficient secretary.

But she really must diet, she thought idly. The extra

seven pounds she had put on over Christmas had stayed with her ever since, and it didn't look good on her smallish frame and medium height. It was hard to diet in the winter, though, when one tended to eat more in an effort to offset the cold. Still, spring was just around the corner. At least, it should be! One wouldn't think so, judging by today's weather.

She kept her speed down, concentrating on her driving and thinking random thoughts at the same time, feeling no particular curiosity about Mr Finn or her prospective assignment. The motorway surface was very slushy and the visibility was poor, so April stayed in the slow lane, glad she had allowed herself plenty of time for the journey. Good old Alan. Sensible Alan. She was glad, now, that he had made her leave so early. One thing she really disliked was unpunctuality.

She was even more grateful to her brother when she got into Buckinghamshire and found herself travelling down narrow country lanes which were becoming more treacherous by the minute. The snow was really sticking here, piling up thickly because there was so little traffic to disperse it.

When she came to an unsignposted T-junction, April drew to a halt and looked at her hand-drawn map. 'Proceed from Great Brickhill, turning left at . . .' She looked helplessly at her own scribble. Was she in Great Brickhill? Or was it ahead of her? Of course, there was nobody about whom she could ask.

It was intuition alone which decided her to turn left, and within minutes she found she was following her map precisely. Ten minutes later, after she had travelled the full length of the road on which Mr Finn's house should be standing, April stopped the car

again. She wasn't perturbed, just mildly frustrated.
This was hardly more than a country lane and the
snow-covered hedges that flanked either side of it were
so high that she couldn't see over them.

She was just getting out of her car when her luck
broke. Coming towards her was a Post Office van, and
she didn't hesitate to flag it down.

'Are you in trouble?' The rosy-faced driver beamed
at her.

'No, no. Just a little lost. I'm looking for Serena
House.' April held up a hand against the wind and the
snow blowing into her eyes.

'It's just along there,' the driver said kindly. 'Drive
another two hundred yards and it's there, on your left.
It's set back off the road a bit, but you'll see the gates.
Cheerio!'

April saw the gates all right. They were wrought-
iron, about twenty feet high and set in the midst of a
brick wall which curved and vanished out of sight to
the left and the right. No wonder she hadn't seen this
from the road, the entrance was set back about a
hundred yards or so. Beyond the gates was an avenue
of poplars flanking the driveway to the house. The
only problem was, how to get on to the driveway?

Edging the car right up to the gates, she was left
with no choice but to get out and investigate, curiosity
stirring within her as she looked up at this ... this
formidable entrance. What was this place—Colditz?

As she got out of the car she saw that there was, in
fact, a brass nameplate set into one of the concrete
posts from which the gates hung. Serena House, it
said simply. What a lovely name for a house! It had
the feeling of peace and tranquillity. But the
nameplate was so small it was almost a shy admission

that the house even existed. Clearly, Mr Finn enjoyed his privacy.

That thought was confirmed when suddenly there appeared, as if from thin air, two full-grown Alsatian dogs on the other side of the gates, barking their heads off and giving her the full view of their teeth.

'Sugar!' April leapt backwards, boggling at the ferocious guard-dogs and very, very grateful that the gates stood between herself and them. How the devil was she supposed to get into this place? Did she *want* to get into this place?

Then from her right, perfectly audible despite the noise the dogs were making, she heard a gruff voice demanding, 'Who's calling?' April's head snapped round, but there was no one to be seen. As the voice repeated itself she registered, feeling something of an idiot, that there was an intercom built into the other gatepost. She walked over to it and spoke clearly into the little grille. 'April Baxter. From the Morrison Agency.'

The gruff voice came back at her. 'Finn speaking. I take it you're in a car?'

'Of course.'

'Then come along. I'll open the gates.'

'What about the dogs?' she blurted.

'Once the gates are released, they won't bother you, Miss Baxter.'

April's gaze went from the intercom to the bared teeth of the Alsatians, and back again. I only hope you're right, she thought, conjuring up a picture of the face belonging to the voice. It occurred to her, of course, that she could do an about-turn and just drive away from this place and this man who had insisted on interviewing her. But April was made of sterner stuff

than that. She was a girl who took everything in her
stride. She was not easily surprised and she was not
easily impressed. Mr Finn was probably wildly
eccentric, she realised, but mightn't that be fun? Mildly
entertaining? It would be interesting. Besides, she was
so curious by now that she was determined to see the
man. She would go through with the interview, at least.

As if they, too, were remote-controlled, the dogs
immediately stopped barking and stood still when the
huge iron gate swung open. There were not two gates,
but one. No wonder April had been unable to see a
latch or a bolt! The gate swung open from the right,
paused, then swung closed and clicked behind her
after she was well clear of it.

She drove slowly along the curving drive, glancing
at the dogs from her driving mirror. They were
sauntering away now, having lost all interest in the
visitor. Visitor? She felt more like an intruder, and was
grateful for the protection of her car. Would those
Alsatians have behaved so well had she been on foot?
Which thought amused her—how on earth did the
postman get on?

No, in this part of the country the post would have
to be delivered by van. Or at least by bicycle. The
houses were so few and far between and the drive to
Serena House alone would have necessitated a fifteen-
minute walk for the fittest person.

The grounds were vast. Not that April could see
much, thanks to the blizzard. Everything was draped
in a thick white blanket so the contents of the gardens
were indiscernible, nothing more than a series of little
humps and hillocks, anonymous. Apart from the trees.
The avenue of poplars was behind her now, but there
were other trees here and there in the foreground,

their shapes making some of them identifiable. In the distance, there were woods. And now, just fifty yards ahead of her, there was the house.

Serena House was Georgian. An elegant Georgian country house in a slightly elevated position. It was gorgeous. The centre front protruded, where the rooms were built with sweeping bays. It was big, by April's standards it was very big—yet by no means as large as its vast grounds had suggested it might be. There were creepers growing over the brickwork at the front, pruned and curving away from the windows so they wouldn't obscure any light.

Two very tall fir trees stood, as if to attention, one on either side of the house, and she drew her car to a halt thinking that the entire setting looked absolutely magical, like something on a Christmas card. Her curiosity about Mr Finn was growing deeper by the minute.

As she dashed up the four stone steps at the front entrance, the snow and wind playing havoc with her usually neat hair, Mr Finn held open the door for her. She knew it was him, although she hadn't expected him personally to admit her to his house; she had expected a butler to do that, or at least a maid. But she knew this was Mr Finn, because she'd put a face to the voice on the intercom and she wasn't far wrong.

It was impossible to guess his age; he could have been fifty, he could have been sixty. His pinkish face was large and round, the top of his head shiny and bald apart from a few strands which were hanging on for dear life. What little hair skirted the rest of his head was cut very short. It might once have been the same dull blonde as April's own hair, but was now salt and pepper.

His eyes were somewhat offputting, inasmuch as they seemed to look right inside her. They were watery, very pale blue and piercing, and just as expressionless as his face. He was wearing a really old-fashioned suit, dark brown and worsted, double-breasted, with a waistcoat and trousers that had turn-ups!

Yes, April thought, just as I expected, he's a real eccentric. She greeted him formally, just in case she was jumping to conclusions and this wasn't the man himself . . .

'Good afternoon. I'm April Baxter. I have an appointment with Mr Finn at three o'clock.'

'I'm Finn,' he said, closing the door behind her. The wind had whooshed into the hall and overhead there was a delicate tinkling sound. April looked up to see a magnificent chandelier hanging from the high ceiling, a myriad colours reflecting off crystal droplets as it shimmered against the sudden draught.

'You're eleven minutes early.' The voice was gruff, though not as much so as it had sounded on the intercom. It was also neutral, so April had no idea whether his comment was admonitory or whether it was praise that she'd managed to get there at all—considering the snow.

Her left hand went automatically to smooth down her hair as she held out her right hand towards him. 'I'm pleased to meet you, Mr Finn. I—er—I understand you require secretarial services? The—the agency . . .' Her voice trailed off. This man was making her feel uncomfortable, though she couldn't pinpoint the reason for it.

He didn't shake hands, he simply said, 'The name's Finn. Just Finn. Your appointment is not with me,

Miss Baxter. I spoke to your agency on my employer's behalf. It is Monsieur le Comte who wishes to interview you. If you will follow me . . .'

April didn't move. Monsieur le Comte? Her prospective employer was French? And a Count at that! She was surprised, there was no denying it. She was also vaguely irritated because she now felt sure she wouldn't take this job even if it were offered. Quite apart from the offputting performance at the entrance to this house, the mention of 'Monsieur le Comte' filled her head with all sorts of new notions. He would be old, very old and decrepit. He would probably be hard of hearing, and crotchety because of it. He would be writing his memoirs, about his life as a member of the French aristocracy.

As for Finn—what was he? The old family retainer? He didn't look like a family retainer. No doubt as strong as an ox, with that very thick-set build and the broadest neck she'd ever seen, he looked more like a retired boxer, or perhaps an ex-policeman. A detective.

Finn turned, waiting for her, and April shook herself mentally for letting her imagination run riot. She was being so silly! But still . . . 'Mr Finn. I mean, Finn—your employer, I understand he's a writer. Is he a biographer, perhaps?'

'No, miss, he's a novelist.' He turned away from her as she blinked in surprise. A novelist, eh? Curiouser and curiouser!

'You say he's a Count. Who is he exactly?'

The watery blue eyes held hers steadily. 'He is Monsieur le Comte Emile Jacquot de Nîmes.' And with that he walked down a corridor leading from the hall, as if he were not prepared to answer any more questions, and leaving April with no choice but to follow him.

'Le Comte Emile Jacquot de Nîmes. Le Comte Emile . . .' April whispered the name to herself as she walked behind Finn, as if it would help her to realise why it sounded familiar. Somewhere in the farthest recesses of her mind a bell was ringing. Quite loudly. She'd heard that name before—but where? And in what context? It had to do with writing, of course. Or had it? No. No, that didn't feel right, even though she knew for a fact that the Count was a writer. She was flummoxed. Flummoxed and very, very intrigued.

Finn came to a halt, opened a door and motioned her inside. 'If you will wait in the drawing room, miss, the Count will see you at three o'clock.'

His further reference to the time made April smile. She might have glanced at her watch to see how many minutes remained before she would be granted an audience, if the room she'd stepped into hadn't been such an enormous distraction.

At Finn's request, she gave him her coat and waited till he had left the room, closing the door noiselessly, before she drank in her surroundings.

April had worked in some very prestigious offices; on several occasions her job had taken her inside the smart houses of wealthy businessmen and women who sometimes worked from home. Indeed, her own parents' house had been very tastefully furnished and decorated. So she was not easily impressed. But this house, this room at least, was something she fell in love with instantly.

It was neither smart nor overstated. Certainly it was expensively furnished, but its contents were so thoughtfully arranged that the first impression it gave was one of cosiness. It was a room which was obviously used and enjoyed, and far from being a showpiece.

The flooring was parquet, two thirds of it covered by a large, square Chinese carpet which was approaching turquoise and had an intricate pattern woven into the corners in beige.

There were two settees set at an L-shaped angle to the creamy-coloured marble fireplace in which there burned a roaring log fire. Facing one of the settees, near the fire, was a high-backed armchair with wings, overstuffed and very comfortable-looking. The Count's chair, perhaps? The one he liked always to sit in?

The walls were the colour of straw, very, very pale. Three lamps were switched on, probably because the day was so dull with the heavy snow clouds, and their faintly golden glow gave an added aura of warmth to the room.

Alas, there was no time to examine things more closely because Finn reappeared in no time at all. Obviously, it was three o'clock precisely! But April had at least glimpsed everything, the mahogany grand piano, the satinwood pier table on which there stood a superb copy of Rodin's sculpture, 'The Kiss'.

Cherchez la femme, she thought. This wasn't the drawing room of an old man living alone. There was definitely a woman's touch here. A woman of breeding, of excellent taste and discernment.

Yes, it was a beautiful room. Welcoming and full of atmosphere. There was also a certain ... April's eyes swept over it once more as she tried to define her impression ... a certain *order* about it. It was something about the placing of things; there was a balance and a neatness in the way they had been set out. The lamps, objects d'art and paintings, even the ashtrays—everything was set in place . . .

Finn was standing in the doorway. 'Miss Baxter, if you will come with me, Monsieur le Comte will see you in the library.'

April followed him into the passageway, astonished to find she was actually feeling nervous. How silly! She might lack confidence in herself as a woman, but she could certainly handle an interview and the demands of her profession!

She clung to that thought, that comforting knowledge, when she set eyes on Le Comte Emile Jacquot de Nîmes. He was sitting behind a massive desk, facing her, his back to the window, and as she followed Finn into the room April had to force herself to keep moving, not to stop in her tracks and stare.

The visit to Serena House had already kept her continually surprised, but all she had experienced and seen so far was as nothing compared to the shock of coming face to face with the Count. To say that he wasn't remotely like what she had imagined would just be further evidence of the English tendency to understate.

To say he was handsome would not be sufficient, either, to describe him. He was stunningly, dramatically attractive, with a lean, beautifully sculptured face and the sort of skin that always looks brown. His hair was slightly unruly, the sideburns a fraction too long. It was thick and straight, as black as night but for two small patches, just below the temples, which looked as if they had been brushed with silvery paint. Premature greyness, it had to be, because the Count could only be in his mid or perhaps late thirties.

A plain black polo-neck sweater added to the darkly dramatic appearance, the fine cashmere fitting closely to a lean but muscular frame. His shoulders were broad and square, and he sat, unsmiling, in an attitude of waiting, with his hands held loosely together on top of the desk, his long fingers intertwined.

He was exceptionally, extraordinarily attractive, and the shock of coming face to face with him took April's breath away. Furthermore, she knew instantly that she was in the presence of a very powerful man. A ruthless man. There was a hardness, a cruelty about the mouth, thin-lipped and unyielding, which left her in no doubt that he was a man who would brook no nonsense, a man who expected, and got, the best of everything in life.

CHAPTER TWO

JET black eyes raked over April as she moved further into the library, the dark head inclined slightly as he watched her. He was not meeting her eye to eye, rather he was summing her up in toto. And April's first, utterly ridiculous thought was a fervent wish that she was a beautiful woman ... a pretty woman ... even attractive. Oh, why hadn't she at least worn some make-up for this interview? Even her professional confidence was deserting her now.

They were standing, she and Finn, just a few feet into the room.

'Monsieur le Comte—Miss Baxter.' Finn motioned her towards one of two padded, dark brown leather chairs which had a circular coffee table between them and were set facing the desk but several yards from it. It was a large room, and April felt glad of the distance between herself and the Count, her stomach becoming knotted with something more than nervousness. There was something vaguely familiar about this man whom she knew she had never met before. No, familiar was too strong a word.

She sat, with a deferential nod in his direction, still having to coach herself not to stare. Luckily, her voice betrayed nothing of her nervousness as she greeted him. 'Monsieur le Comte ...'

Finn was still hovering as she seated herself. Then he did something which struck April as being rather odd: he picked up her handbag from where she had put it—on the table between the two chairs—and placed it carefully underneath the table. She glanced at him curiously, thinking this was taking tidiness too far, but Finn's large and pinkish face remained expressionless.

Only when Finn had left the room did the Count Emile Jacquot de Nîmes get down to business. 'Miss Baxter, there are two things I dislike intensely— mediocrity and indecision.'

April's eyes widened. His voice was liquid, the French accent very slight. It was deep and calm but with varying shades. It made her think of dark brown velvet, always rich, always smooth, but with a changing appearance if one brushed a finger across the pile or held it up to the light.

It did not deceive her. April was working on intuition alone, but her intuition was something which rarely let her down. The voice was deliberately controlled. With its trace of accent and its depth, it was undeniably attractive but it could mask at will a hundred emotions. She looked at him, fascinated and even slightly afraid, and stupid though it might have been, all she could think in that instant was that she wouldn't like to be around if this man ever lost his temper.

She didn't know what to say, if anything. His remark had taken her by surprise. It was by no means the way interviews normally began! He was stating facts—was he expecting a comment?

She looked at him blankly as he continued. 'Efficiency and punctuality are two things I do like, however, and it would seem you have both these qualities, in view of your punctual arrival after driving through a blizzard.'

Not really understanding him, April played it by
ear. She was a little surprised that as he spoke to her
he did not meet her eyes, although he was looking at
her. In other people, April's reaction to that was
always a suspicion that they were not being strictly
honest, or had something to hide. But she couldn't
think in those terms as far as the Count was
concerned; he was being extremely direct, and if he
did have something to hide it was certainly nothing to
do with interviewing her!

'I drive efficiently, yes. And punctuality is the
politeness of kings. I'm always punctual, Monsieur
le Comte, and I expect it of other people.' She
paused. 'I don't always get it, but I expect it.'
She was thinking hard, unsure what he expected of
her. 'As for mediocrity and indecision, you will find
neither of those traits in me as far as my work is
concerned.'

'I have no doubt that your work will be of the
highest standard,' he informed her then. 'You work
for the Morrison Agency, so we need say no more
about your qualifications. But you are not the first
person they have sent along for this job, nor are you
the second. You are the fifth, Miss Baxter. The *fifth*.
The business of finding myself a new secretary is
proving more time-consuming—and boring—than I'd
anticipated.'

With that, April was thrown into considerable
confusion. This man, so vital, so aristocratic, had such
... such *presence* ... that it was difficult for her to
concentrate. She was not overawed because he was a
Count, but by the enormous power which emanated
from him, enveloping her and creating a distraction.
She was only vaguely aware of her surroundings, of

the crackle and glow of the fire, of walls lined with books from ceiling to floor.

Apart from having to cope with the sheer impact of the man, his news that he had rejected four people from Morrison's was something she could make no sense of. To get on to Morrison's books one had to be tip-top. Maybe they'd rejected him? Highly probable. The Count would not be the easiest person to get along with. But oh, wasn't that a challenge! And April was in need of a challenge.

Beyond those thoughts, in the farthest recesses of her mind there was still this niggling feeling that Le Comte Emile Jacquot de Nîmes was well known for something other than writing. Something April found exciting. She was longing for that part of the interview when he would talk about his work. Perhaps, then, everything would be made clear. He was a novelist, Finn said, but one thing was certain: April had not read anything he'd written. She was a voracious reader of novels, and she would have remembered . . . unless he used a pen-name.

If only she could go away, sort everything out in her mind, absorb the—the shock—of this encounter, then come back and start this interview afresh!

'Forgive me,' she said, blushing to the roots as she realised she'd been staring at him. 'I'm not normally tongue-tied, I assure you.' A nervous laugh escaped her, just a slight release of tension. 'But I don't understand you. With respect, Monsieur le Comte, if you feel certain my work will be satisfactory, why did you deem it necessary to interview me? And what happened with the other people from——'

'Because I am very particular about the people, about the *personalities*, with whom I work.' She could sense his irritation, though his voice gave no indication of it. 'I would be booking your services for six months, give or take a couple of weeks. Quite apart from that, you would be living under my roof, and of necessity I am extremely cautious about any person who moves into my home.'

April looked down at her hands, her mouth making an involuntary clicking sound as she fought not to show her annoyance. She was slow to anger, but this news had succeeded in doing just that. Boy, would she give Phyllis a piece of her mind first thing Monday morning! Fancy not telling April that this was a living-in job. Its duration wasn't particularly important, but she might at least have told her she'd be expected to live in! It didn't matter one way or the other to April, she was free to do as she pleased, but this interview would have started a damn sight more successfully if she'd been forewarned of the Count's requirements. Of his existence, even! As far as she'd known, her interview was with a Mr Finn. Damn Phyllis and her haste to get away for the weekend. Her lack of information was making April look foolish now! And April wanted this assignment, to work with this fascinating, challenging man, more than she had wanted anything in a long time. She had made her mind up on that as soon as she'd walked into the library.

But it was going to be far more difficult than she'd imagined. And here she was, sitting like a confused idiot, whilst the Count waited expectantly, his dark brows drawn together in a frown.

Her loyalty to her agency prevented her from telling the Count she hadn't been given full details about the job, especially since he didn't seem too pleased with Morrison's as it was! But she started talking, fast.

'Yes, I understand. Well, I can assure you of two things. I have the ability to adapt, both to my surroundings and to my boss's pace of work. Your home is very beautiful, from what I've seen of it so far. I would respect it. That, and the fact that you obviously enjoy the quiet life, the emphasis being on privacy.'

His look of concentration was so intense that it made her even more selfconscious. Conscious of every word she spoke, conscious of her plainness, and acutely conscious that she was about to be his fifth rejection.

Judging by what she had seen of his home, this man enjoyed being surrounded by things that were pleasing to the eye. Something April was not. Nor did she have the sort of personality which could override her plainness.

When the Count got up from his desk April thought this brief and formal interview was finished. She was astonished when he offered her a drink.

'May I offer you a glass of wine, Miss Baxter? Or would you prefer a hot drink—perhaps you'd prefer tea?'

'Oh, thank you. Er—is that brandy, in one of those decanters?'

'Cognac, yes.'

'Then I'll have cognac, if I may. Just a small one. I'm driving.'

The offer, the gesture, helped April to relax slightly, but his walk, his movements, kept her half-hypnotised. Who *was* this man? Where had she seen him before? On the television? Anywhere, in fact?

She watched him as he stood with his back half turned to her. She could see, now, that his slacks were also black, immaculately cut and fitting closely enough to reveal powerful thigh muscles. Tall and lean, the Count obviously kept himself in perfect condition, for there wasn't an ounce of excess flesh on the broad and muscular frame.

He was pouring two glasses of cognac with movements which were deliberate and precise, as if he thought about everything before he made a move. He probably does, April mused. He had told her himself that he was a cautious man. She admired and envied his supreme confidence. There was an aura of total calm and control about him, something it seemed would be impossible to disturb. And yet—and yet . . .

As he walked towards her, glasses in hand, April knew that same uneasiness she had felt as she had registered the cruelty in the set of his mouth. In more than the physical sense, there was a strength about him which was harnessed. Tightly harnessed. His movements were easy, fluid, but they made April think of a black panther, striding silently with all his senses alert; watching, waiting.

To her utter dismay he set both glasses on the table and sat in the chair beside hers. She was fazed, fascinated, excited and disturbed. From such close range she could see a scar, no more than the breadth of a hair, running from the silvery patch of hair at his right temple to the outer edge of his eyebrow. It was not a scar from his childhood days, but it was old enough to have faded somewhat, and whoever had stitched it had been a master.

He was looking directly at her now, the black eyes locked on to hers with such piercing clarity she felt sure he would be able to read her mind, see into her soul. She managed a smile, wondering what on earth it would take to draw a smile from him.

'Did your agency tell you anything about my routine?' he asked. 'About the hours of work and so on?'

April hedged slightly. 'Er—no. They didn't go into the finer details.'

'Then let me fill you in before we go any further.' He took a sip of his drink. 'I start dictation at seven in the morning. That's why I need someone who's prepared to live in. I like to work in the early morning, the best part of the day. That's when the mind is fresh, before there are any aggravations, such as phone calls. I don't even open my post until I've finished my day's work.

'I finish dictating around eleven o'clock, usually. Finn serves lunch at one-thirty. Dinner is served at eight. I don't care when the day's dictation is typed up. That would be up to you—whether you leave your afternoons free and do it in the evening, or vice versa. I work on Saturdays but not on Sundays. All I ask is that the previous day's dictation is typed ready for the following morning. Your weekends, therefore, would be slightly shortened, but you would still have Saturday afternoon and Sunday free, depending on how you would choose to work.'

April nodded. 'How many staff live in?'

'Just Finn. I live alone, apart from him. I employ several gardeners, local people. And that's it. Finn runs the house. And you would have the freedom of the house, just as long as you respect my privacy. I think you'll have gathered by now that I'm something of a hermit. Haven't you, Miss Baxter?'

His voice, the slight accent, really was a pleasure to hear. He pronounced her name 'Baxteur'.

April was thinking of the neatness of the drawing room, those touches she had interpreted as being a woman's influence. Since the Count lived alone, Finn must be responsible for that. Of course! Hadn't he tidied her handbag away as soon as she had sat down? Finn—no, the Count—must be extremely particular about tidiness!

She was more than intrigued by this man, and longing to ask him about his novels. But it was too soon for that. Firstly, he wanted to establish whether she would be prepared to work to his somewhat eccentric hours. Well, it made no difference to her what hours she worked. And she would still be able to visit Alan and the children at weekends.

'Your hesitation speaks volumes,' he said then. 'Am I to take it you're no longer interested in the job?'

'Not at all!' she blurted. 'I'm sorry, it's just that "hermit" is not the word I'd have chosen. I—I'd rather say that you choose to live quietly and your privacy is of paramount importance.'

'Indeed?' There was a slight pull at the corners of his mouth, the promise of a smile which never got started. 'You dislike the connotations of the word hermit?'

She glanced at him then looked away. What a puzzle he was! There were many, many layers to him. As a writer he must be perceptive. And he would be careful in choosing his words; 'hermit' was not chosen by accident. But she didn't want to think of him as a hermit. He was not the crotchety old man she had once fancied him to be. Far from it! He was vital and alive and—oh, what a waste it would be if the world never set eyes on him. For womankind, at least!

'Pertaining to you,' she answered boldly, honestly, 'yes.'

There was a moment's silence. Then he lifted his glass and downed the contents in one go. 'Tell me, Mademoiselle, are you an optimist or a pessimist?'

April didn't hesitate. 'Neither. I'm a realist.'

'Is that so?' There was just the slightest hint of amusement in his voice, but not even the promise of a smile. 'Tell me about yourself.'

She was just beginning to understand him. He was a prospective employer, but no ordinary man. He didn't want her name, rank and number. He wanted to know what she was made of, how she thought, what her attitudes to life were. Tell me about yourself, he'd said. What a daunting, inhibiting request when she was such an ordinary, run-of-the-mill person. There was nothing interesting about her life, or her personality.

Consequently, April gave him brief details, even knowing that this would not satisfy him. 'I'm April Baxter. Twenty-three years old. Brought up in the country with one brother who's a lot older than I. Now living in Paddington, London, in my own flat.'

The room was growing dark as the afternoon wore on. She wished the Count would move away, go back to his desk. His nearness was difficult to cope with, and in this light there was an almost sinister look about him.

'You haven't touched your drink, Miss Baxter. If you don't relax a little, we shall continue to get nowhere.' Despite the calm, velvet voice she knew he was irritated with her. He paused, and April wondered why he didn't say goodbye there and then.

'April—*Avril*,' he mused, translating her name into the French, 'so named because you were born during that month, I suppose?'

She giggled nervously, 'No. Oh, that was the theory, but Mummy got her timing wrong. I was born on the first of May! Still, I'm glad she didn't change her mind and call me May.'

'Tell me, what do you do with your evenings?'

'I read a lot,' she said, hoping they would stay on the subject of books.

But the Count just passed over it. 'You have no commitments? A fiancé or a boy-friend who would grumble because you would be stuck out in the country during the week?'

'No.'

'When do you go out? At weekends? What do you do for entertainment?'

'If I don't go to my brother's straight from work, then I go out. Fridays, that is.'

'And what do you do then?' he probed.

'I go to the theatre. Preferably the ballet or the opera.' She paused. 'I—It's my own treat after a hard week's work.'

He picked her up on that. 'Your own treat? Does that mean you go alone?'

'I—er——' She shifted uneasily, forcing herself to uncross her arms and her legs. If the Count knew anything at all about body language, he'd see she was answering his questions unwillingly. Which was rather silly of her, really, since he wasn't getting *too* personal. But it would be a difficult admission, letting him know that more often than not she was alone on Friday evenings. It would imply that she was not only without a boy-friend, but friendless, too. And that wasn't the case. She had girl-friends. It was just that most of them were married now, apart from Shirley, who was her closest friend. She had known Shirley since she had first started at Morrison's and they had hit it off together from the start. The trouble was that Shirley had recently got engaged and was less inclined to go out these days because she was saving her money for a house deposit.

April passed on that one, volunteering other information in the hope that his questions would lead in another direction. 'Every other weekend I visit my brother. He—he's a widower, you see. He—he lives in Surrey and has two children. I—as a matter of fact, I came from there today.'

But the Count Emile Jacquot de Nîmes was not easily distracted. 'What about dancing—nightclubs? This doesn't sound right, Miss Baxter. Here you are, a young woman living in the most exciting city in the world, apart from Paris, so why aren't you having the time of your life?'

Now he was getting too personal. And she was getting slightly annoyed. Or was he being deliberately cruel? He could see for himself she wasn't the world's greatest beauty, wasn't even the sort of girl whose evenings would be booked well in advance.

She lowered her eyes, away from his steady gaze and on to his mouth. Yes, he was more than capable of deliberate, calculated cruelty. Why didn't she terminate this interview—this third degree—right now?

She didn't. She couldn't even answer her own question. Instead she picked up her drink, took a big swallow—and gagged on it immediately. The Count waited patiently while she coughed and spluttered, gasping, excusing herself—and feeling an absolute idiot.

'Why are you so lacking in confidence?' he asked at length, when her coughing had died away. Then, with a dismissive wave of an arm, 'Never mind. Tell me, are you squeamish—easily shocked?'

April realised he had been leading her, probing, trying to discover what sort of person she was, but she could see no relevance at all in his last question.

Right now, she ought to leave. She knew that. She should tell him she'd changed her mind, lost interest. But that wouldn't be true. The content of his work had grown more and more irrelevant as time went on. Her interest was in the man himself. When there was other work available for one with her qualifications, she didn't need this job. She didn't need it, but she wanted it. She was caught, captured by what could only be described as his sheer magnetism. And the fascination grew and grew; from his strange line of questioning April was learning a few things, too. She was getting just a slight understanding of the surface layers of the man. And there were plenty more underneath. Plenty. She knew that as surely as she knew that that bell was still ringing in her head.

She risked looking at him then, shrivelling inwardly but outwardly appearing to withstand the appraisal from eyes as dark as night. It was then, as he waited for her to speak, that she realised she must be totally honest with him. For him, nothing less would do. He simply wanted her to be herself. She must relax, and be just that. If she didn't live up to his requirements, nebulous though they remained, then it would be hard luck—for her.

Drawing a deep breath, she met his gaze as she spoke. 'I begin to understand you, Monsieur le Comte. You want an assurance that I won't become bored being here. You have it. There'd be no swapping and changing secretaries. I would see this

assignment through to the end. Six months, you say—
that's presumably the time it will take to write your
novel.

'You see, the idea of living in the country again
appeals to me very much. The grounds of your
house are no doubt magnificent, when they're visible!
At the moment they look like something off the
front of a Christmas card, somehow unreal—and
beautiful. I'd enjoy walking in those grounds in my
free time. Exploring, watching them change with the
seasons . . .'

Her voice trailed off as she saw the intense look of
concentration which had settled on his face, just as it
had earlier. What she wanted to say next was difficult.
'I—you—you can see for yourself that I'm neither
glamorous nor the flighty type. There's nothing in
London, in the form of dancing, nightclubs or . . . or
men . . . that I would miss. Like yourself, I enjoy the
quiet life.

'I realise you've been quizzing me, trying to draw
me out, but it's making me nervous. And all you really
want to know is whether I'm reliable. Well, my agency
can vouch not only for my abilities but also for my
integrity and trustworthiness.

'Frankly, I see no sense in your last question, but
I'll answer it just the same. No, I'm not squeamish,
and after working for two years as a shorthand writer
in the law courts, I'm no longer easily shocked. I'm
not even surprised by the things people do, or what
they do to each other.' She halted abruptly, realising
her little speech had turned into something of a
tirade. It was the result of incomplete understanding,
of the strain and tension she had been under for too
long.

She'd probably made a complete mess of it now. This man wasn't only a client, he was an aristocrat, and no doubt unused to being spoken to like this. If for nothing else he would reject her now for her sheer impertinence.

There was a long, drawn-out silence. April looked out of the window at the rapidly darkening sky. The wind had dropped considerably, but the snow was still falling. It seemed an age before the Count finally spoke.

'Well done,' he said. 'I assure you I have good reason for asking these questions. All of them. As for the last one—you see, my books get very explicit—er—shall we say graphic, in parts. If you were the type of woman who can't bear to hear about blood and bullets, violence in its rawest form, this job would not be for you.'

Blood and bullets? She looked at his mouth. Violence in its rawest form? April's eyes flitted swiftly over his face, the fine scar at his temple, the straight, finely chiselled nose, the arch of black eyebrows, then back again to the thin-lipped, cruel and unyielding mouth. In the fading light his skin looked even darker, lending an almost menacing look to his features. It was a strong face, lean and undeniably beautiful. It was the face of a deep and mysterious man.

'Who are you?' she asked quietly. 'You obviously use a pen-name, Monsieur le Comte. Have we reached the stage now when you're prepared to tell me what it is?'

'We have,' he said. 'It's Jason Jordan.'

He got up then, a tall dark figure striding silently towards the massive antique desk.

Jason Jordan. She'd heard of him, of course. Almost everyone was familiar with that name. As far as April knew, he'd written several books, and his last two were blockbusters—international bestsellers. She hadn't read any of them. They were not her cup of tea. But she could see them, in her mind's eye, in one of those big cardboard display cases they had in the bookshops she spent so many hours in.

She had also seen copies of them in Alan's house. They were stories of violence, about mercenaries— men who fought wars for money—and were more suitable for male readership, in April's opinion.

'Would you like a cigarette?' The Count picked up a silver box from the corner of his desk.

'No, thank you.'

'You don't smoke?'

'Very occasionally, but I won't have one now, thanks.' She paused, knowing she ought to say something about his work. But the truth was, his revelation had left her feeling acutely unsatisfied. Oh, it was interesting, and the man known as Jason Jordan was certainly a master at his craft, but the mystery April had been privately battling with ever since she had heard his real name was not yet solved.

That this man was Jason Jordan, internationally acclaimed author of extremely popular books, all fitted. The impression she had got of his supreme control, a sort of restrained anger, all this was probably given free rein in his violent novels. There was nothing sensitive in that writing, just as there was nothing sensitive about its author. Yes, it all fitted. So why hadn't that bell stopped ringing? Why was she still thinking there was yet another identity to this man?

Because I'm being fanciful, she told herself, I'm making some sort of whopping mistake and I've got my wires crossed somewhere along . . .

'Are you going to keep me waiting all day?' The deceptively smooth voice broke into her thoughts. 'I'm expecting some sort of comment.'

'Oh! Yes. Sorry!' April struggled to focus her concentration. 'I'm afraid I haven't read your books. But I'm familiar with their nature,' she added lamely.

Emile Jacquot de Nîmes shrugged as if he couldn't care less. 'I want to know if you'd be happy to work with that sort of material.'

Then it was her turn to shrug. 'Why not? I mean, it's only fiction, isn't it?'

He let out a long, slow breath. Relief that he'd finally found a suitable and reliable secretary? Impatience? Disagreement with her remark?

'If there really is such a thing. Miss Baxter, there are a couple more things I'd like to cover before either of us can make a decision. I need someone to start work immediately, on Monday . . .' As he spoke, he moved over to the fireplace, and in the momentary release from his scrutiny April relaxed a little more, her eyes sweeping around the library for the first time.

This room spoke of wealth, with its dark red Persian carpet, its antique furniture and its books. There were so many of them! Hundreds of lovely books!

' . . I've almost reached the end of chapter one in my current novel, and breaking off for several days while I've been trying to find a new secretary has been frustrating, and bad for the book. I take it you'd be free to . . .'

The Count continued to talk, but April simply stopped hearing him. Her mind was suddenly thrown into total chaos, her eyes wide with shock as her gaze came to rest on that which triggered a very elusive memory. Above the fireplace, where the Count was now standing, was an original painting she had seen once before. Just once. A long time ago.

From this distance the artist's signature wasn't legible, but she didn't need to read it. She knew who had painted it; the style was unmistakable, unique, brilliant. And the artist's name was Jacquot.

Jacquot! Of course! Oh, *of course!*

Her devastated gaze was locked on to the painting as incomplete memories raced through her mind like pieces of a jigsaw puzzle . . . the article she had seen in the magazine . . . the background information it had given . . . his photograph—several photographs!

In split seconds everything fell into place and the pieces formed a complete picture, a complete recollection. She gasped, rising slowly from her chair, her voice barely more than a whisper.

'My God! You're blind!' Then she floundered, realising how tactless she sounded when all she really wanted was to let him know she had recognised him, that she had so much admired his work. 'I'm sorry, Monsieur le Comte, it's just that I so much admired your work. I have a reproduction of "An Orchard in Versailles", and I just wanted to say . . .'

Her voice trailed off. She was being a tactless, bungling idiot. The painting she had referred to was the last one Jacquot had completed before he had been struck by the tragedy which had robbed him of his sight, and the world of a great artist.

April sank back into her chair, her face growing crimson with embarrassment as other memories, very recent memories, tumbled into place. She was squirming inwardly, thinking of the things she had said—things she would never have dreamt of saying if she had realised he was blind!

The Count had turned away from her. The skin on his knuckles was white as he gripped the mantelpiece with both hands, fighting for control. This had never happened before. Other strangers, the other interviewees, had not recognised him—or his paintings—and he had thought himself safe from this sort of trespass.

He was a fool. A fool to run the risk of recognition, a recognition which brought only pain. But it would never happen again! Tonight he would strip the house of his paintings—all of them.

Fool! Again, fool. If only he *could* do that.

The more immediate problem was this girl. It would be a pity to let her go, this girl who spoke of Christmas cards and watching the changing seasons. But he had to let her go. She had recognised him, she had been an admirer, and he could not bear the attitude, the *pity* which would inevitably contaminate their working relationship. He must get rid of her. Now.

April had wondered why he hadn't told her who he really was. She had wondered why he hadn't at least told her of his blindness. Indeed, why hadn't she seen it for herself? But, watching him during the long silence, she had answered her own questions, had come to realise a few things for herself . . .

. . . Her recognition of him as a painter was the last thing the Count had wanted. He had turned away from her not when she mentioned his blindness, but as soon as she mentioned his painting. That told her all she needed to know: his life as a painter must not be mentioned again.

But his blindness was something he had long since overcome, so she need feel no embarrassment at the things she had said. Indeed, he had wanted her to be herself, to behave and speak naturally, without being inhibited by any prior knowledge.

Casting around in her mind, she wondered how she could show him that she understood how it was with him. She was filled with an overwhelming respect for the Count, not only as a man who had mastered a severe handicap but as an artist who was still able to give pleasure and entertainment to people, albeit, nowadays, in an entirely different way.

Whether she got the job or not, she simply had to finish this interview on the right note. What her intuition was now telling her to say at first seemed almost brutal, but she knew it was right.

Taking a deep breath to steady herself, April spoke in a businesslike manner, her voice showing not the slightest trace of emotion. 'Sorry for getting sidetracked. Having made my acknowledgement to Jacquot, I can now forget about him and get on with the business in hand. But it's getting rather dark in here, and while I realise it makes no difference to you, it would be far more comfortable for me if you'd switch on the lamps while we finish the interview.'

As the Count turned slowly to face her, April's heart was in her mouth. Had she gone too far with her bluntness?

Emile Jacquot de Nîmes was momentarily stuck for words. Then he grinned, and the grin developed into a smile that changed his entire countenance, chasing away all the shadows of his face, lighting his dark eyes and revealing strong white teeth. April's breath caught in her throat. This was like the sun suddenly appearing from behind a dark cloud on a midsummer's day.

'The interview is finished,' he said. 'The job is yours.'

CHAPTER THREE

APRIL'S hands were still trembling slightly as she poured boiling water into her small teapot. She should phone Alan immediately, explain that she wouldn't be returning to Surrey. She should do the washing, clean up the flat, give the flowers she'd bought only yesterday to the old lady who lived down the hall. Tomorrow she would be moving into Serena House, and there were lots of things that needed her attention.

But instead of getting on with her chores she sat by the gas fire in the living room of her one-bedroomed flat. She couldn't phone Alan yet, couldn't do anything until she sorted out her feelings and thoughts which were the aftermath of her meeting with the Count Emile Jacquot de Nîmes ... Jason Jordan, the writer ... Jacquot, the painter.

What an extraordinary, fascinating man! She had thought him so from the start, before she knew his pen-name, before she knew who he really was. That was a thought. Who was he—really? She shook her head, still bewildered by the day's events. He was a man of many layers. For the moment, she could say no more than that. She simply could not reconcile the man she had met with the artist who had created such beautiful, romantic paintings.

In her assessment of him during the interview she had thought him insensitive. How wrong could she be? Her eyes travelled over to that which was her proudest possession, a reproduction of the last painting Jacquot had completed. It was set in an orchard at the height of summer and depicted a young couple strolling hand in hand through the trees. The girl was wearing a blue broderie anglaise dress, full length, and a broad picture hat with flowers on the brim. The young man was dressed in white; the smile on his face, the look in his eyes a silent pronouncement of the love he felt for his companion.

Did it represent Jacquot himself, in his younger days? Jacquot, and the girl he married? Oh, yes, the Count was married. April remembered that from the article she had read about him. The photographs it showed of him and his wife had made her think what a beautiful couple they made. His wife was stunning.

It had all happened five years ago, in the year during which Liz had died. In the winter of that year April had persuaded Alan to accompany her to the first British exhibition of the paintings of a relatively unknown French artist. Relatively unknown in England, that was. Really it had been an attempt to provide Alan with a change of scenery, an attempt to take him out of himself.

Alan had traipsed around the gallery showing no interest at all. April, on the other hand, had fallen in love with almost everything she saw. Jacquot's paintings were gentle, exquisitely romantic. She had bought her reproduction then; an original was way beyond her means. Even the reproduction had taken most of her savings. Not that she cared, because she was already earning good money in the courts.

The exhibition had been tremendously well received and attended, perhaps more so than the gallery had expected because of the publicity in the newspapers about the accident in which Jacquot had been involved on the day before the preview. He had been flying from France to England in a private plane which had made a crash landing in a field somewhere down south.

So it was that at the time of the exhibition Jacquot had been lying unconscious in a London hospital bed. Nobody knew, then, that the painter had lost his sight. That was reported in the New Year, in the full-feature article April saw in a Sunday newspaper magazine. It had read almost like an obituary. It had mentioned the Count's full name, but he was known in the art world simply as Jacquot.

No wonder April hadn't recognised him sooner than she did. Five years was a long time, and being introduced to him as a writer had thrown her completely.

These days Jacquot's paintings were no doubt worth a great deal of money; one never read of them changing hands, one never heard his name mentioned. His paintings were probably in private collections in several countries, appreciating in value not only with the passage of time but because their number could never be increased; as far as the world of art was concerned, Jacquot was dead.

But the Count Emile Jacquot de Nîmes was very much alive. So was Jason Jordan.

April sighed, trying to force her mind back to the present. Her recollections of the Count's tragedy had made her feel extremely sad.

But what a tremendous, admirable adjustment he had made. Not only as far as his career was concerned. She could have worked for him for days and never guessed he was totally blind. Except that he would have told her in due course, she knew that. And there had been so many clues—the way everything was set out so neatly in the drawing room, the way he could not meet her eyes until he was quite close to her, his deliberate movements, the way Finn had tidied her bag away, probably so the Count would know exactly where everything was.

April shook her head in amazement at the memory of it all. Emile Jacquot de Nîmes was an extremely clever and superior man. Working for him, she felt certain, would not be merely a job but a unique and valuable experience. She felt inexplicably happy at the prospect.

Her brother answered the phone at the first ring. 'April? Thank heavens! I was getting quite worried. Where are you?'

'At home.'

'Oh, well, I don't blame you. It would've been potty to drive down here in this weather. How did you get on at the interview? Did he like the look of you?'

It seemed like an extremely tactless question, but it was a natural one, especially in view of April's parting shot to him.

'I—er—evidently he did.'

Alan chuckled. 'You don't sound too sure.'

April smiled wryly. 'Well, I got the job.' She went on to explain that she would be moving into Serena House the following day, and the reason for that. More than that, she didn't tell her brother, although he did ask whether her new employer was a well-known writer.

'Yes,' she said, 'he is. But he seems to be very obsessive about concealing his identity and guarding his privacy, so I can't tell you his pen-name over the phone.' Come to think of it, she wouldn't be able to tell anyone outside the agency, unless the Count gave his permission.

With an assurance that she would see him the following weekend, plus explicit instructions on how to cook tomorrow's roast beef, April finished the call. And not without reminding him to place his advertisement for a housekeeper.

At eleven o'clock she got out of the bath, having had a long soak, sung three of her favourite songs from 'The Sound of Music', and washed her hair. Singing in the bath was a habit she'd never grown out of.

The washing and ironing was done, the flat was spotless, the milk cancelled, and she had even made a mental list of the clothes she would be taking to Serena House.

April's last job of the day was somewhat daunting. For as long as she could remember, she had kept a diary. Perhaps it was pointless, but it was something she did automatically, a deeply ingrained habit. As a teenager she had had ideas of some day writing the story of her life, the diaries being an aide-memoire. Now, however, she realised that that was silly—what boring reading it would make! Still, she continued to make her daily entries, usually just one or two lines.

Tonight was different. Tonight she would need a supplementary piece of paper, despite the fact that she kept her diary in shorthand! She paused, tapping her pencil lightly against her teeth. How on earth to describe the man who had been on her mind all evening? Where should she begin? The first sentence was the most difficult. After that her record flowed very easily. It was turned midnight when she went to bed.

'If there's anything you need, miss, just pick up the telephone and press the buzzer. It works as an intercom to the kitchen, as well as having an outside line.' Finn was wearing the same ghastly suit he had worn the previous day. April glanced from him to the telephone and back again, nodding, and feeling quite bewildered.

Her 'bedroom' had turned out to be a suite of rooms comprising a dressing room, a sitting room (with a three-piece suite, a colour television and even a stereo), and a large bedroom with a bathroom en suite. It was gorgeous. Apart from the sitting room, which had a green Regency-striped wallpaper and a dark green carpet, the suite was done in lilac and white. The walls were of the palest shade of lilac, which was picked up again in the bedspread. The furniture was fitted, white, as were the carpets, ankle-deep and luxurious.

It was far more than April had expected. Even though the Count had told her she would have the freedom of the house, surely this meant that she would actually be expected to stay in her own quarters during her free time? There was, after all, everything she needed here.

This thought was confirmed when Finn said he would bring dinner to her sitting room at eight o'clock. 'Monsieur le Comte starts work at seven,' he said, in his gruff but neutral voice. 'At what time would you like breakfast? And what will you have?'

April sat on the bed, looking up at the pale blue, watery eyes and the inscrutable face. 'Er—just tea and toast for me, please. Would—would it be more convenient for me to have breakfast in the kitchen?'

He didn't even shrug. Blandly he said it was all the same to him, he'd be just as pleased to bring breakfast to her.

'All right. Six o'clock, then. Thank you, Finn.'

She thought he would leave her then, but he picked up her suitcase and placed it on the bed beside her. 'Perhaps you'd care to come down to the kitchen, after you've unpacked, so I can show you where everything is.'

April smiled and nodded, not really understanding the reason for his invitation but perfectly willing to go along with him.

'You see, Miss Baxter, it's very important that everything is kept in its proper place in this house. Monsieur le Comte knows every detail of the house and its grounds. You will understand that it could cause him much inconvenience, could even be dangerous, if things are not put back where they belong. There will be times when you'll help yourself to things from the kitchen. If there were knives lying around, or perhaps a glass left——'

'Ah, yes. Yes, I see.' April's face was solemn as the implications came home to her. 'I'll bear this in mind constantly, I assure you. Don't worry.'

'It's very easy to forget, miss, so please do. I would also ask you always to ensure that doors are closed behind you, never left ajar.'

April looked at him warily. Despite the cool politeness as he told her these things, she had the distinct feeling that Finn would be very unpleasant to contend with if she slipped up in this respect.

With an almost imperceptible nod, he moved towards the door.

'Finn, have you—have you been with the Count a long time?'

'On and off, I have known him all his life.'

On and off? What was that supposed to mean? Really, getting information out of this man was like trying to get blood out of a stone. 'Are you aware that I know who he really is?'

April wasn't really sure why she asked this question, why it seemed so important. Actually, there was much she would have liked to ask Finn, if only his attitude were not so offputting.

He turned, meeting her eyes, seeming to consider his words carefully before he replied. 'He told me, Miss Baxter, that you know who he was.'

She stared at the door after he had closed it behind him. '. . . you know who he *was*.' Who had changed the tense, Finn or the Count? Not that it mattered. Either way, it spoke volumes. It well and truly confirmed her thoughts at the end of yesterday's interview: the Count wished his past to remain dead and buried.

At ten o'clock April switched off the television and decided to do the sensible thing—have an early night. Come to think of it, ten o'clock would become her normal bedtime for the next six months, in view of the early start.

She hadn't seen the Count. He had neither greeted her nor sent any form of message via Finn. Obviously, he simply took it for granted that she would appear in his library on the dot of seven tomorrow morning.

After winding up her travelling alarm clock, she leaned back against the soft pillows, diary in hand, and tried to put her thoughts into some semblance of order. She wrote, 'Today I moved into Serena House, and I have named the manservant "The Inscrutable

Finn!" I have no idea whether he approves or disapproves of me. Not that it matters, I'm just here to do a job . . .'

She paused, pondering over the last sentence. Yes, she was here simply to do a a job, so what was it that was making her feel slightly uneasy, deep down inside? Was it the presence of Finn, that stocky bear of a man with such piercing eyes? Perhaps it was the suspicion that the Count was going to be difficult to get along with—too difficult?

No. It was neither of those things, because in actual fact that vague feeling of uneasiness was tinged with something . . . something approaching excitement.

April wrote this down, then immediately crossed it out. She was being silly. Besides, she thought, the feeling, was far too nebulous to be put into words. Furthermore, nothing at all had been said, either by Finn or his employer, which should make her feel in the least uneasy.

This analysis helped dispel the feeling, and with a dismissive shake of her head she finished her short entry with just one more sentence. In an effort to capture succinctly how she was now feeling—detached, open-minded, neutral—she wrote: 'Colour me white'.

But the shock she experienced on coming face to face with the Count early the next day resurrected instantly the feeling she thought she had dispelled. He was sitting in the leather swivel chair pushed back slightly from his desk, half turned towards the window so that April was struck first by his strong, clear-cut profile.

This morning, looking towards the east where an insipid sun was slowly rising, his eyes appeared to be grey, bleak, and the silvery wings at his temples made a dramatic contrast against hair which was otherwise almost blue-black.

He was wearing black again, plain slacks and an open-necked corduroy shirt which revealed the strong lines of his throat and the growth of dark hair at the top of his chest.

April felt her stomach contract. It had returned, if indeed it had really left her, this vague feeling of uneasiness tinged with—yes, it was excitement. She chided herself for it, for being so affected by his striking handsomeness.

As she closed the door behind her she saw the fingers of his right hand brush lightly over his watch.

'You are punctual, Miss Baxter, as I expected. Your rooms are satisfactory, I trust?'

'More than satisfactory. Thank you.' She paused in the centre of the room, the light from the log fire dappling across her plain blue dress, noting that the chair she had occupied during the interview had been moved. It was next to the massive desk, immediately facing him.

With a typically continental gesture, Emile Jacquot de Nîmes waved her towards it. 'Sit down. We'll start work—have a break for coffee around nine o'clock.'

April sat nervously, astonished at the way he could meet her eyes so accurately when she was close to him, as yet unused to the idea that he could not, in fact, see her.

'Can you read someone else's shorthand?' he asked. 'My last secretary left very abruptly as a result of a family crisis, and the last few pages of the manuscript have not yet been transcribed. It's my habit to hear the last two or three pages before I continue dictating.'

'Let me have a look. It'll depend on how many short

cuts she takes. Most—most shorthand writers develop their own little idiosyncrasies.'

'You mean they deviate from the rules.'

She smiled. 'I mean they deviate from the rules.'

He picked up a reporter's notebook from the desk. 'Why does the idea amuse you?'

April blinked, surprised and impressed at the way he had read the smile in her voice. 'I—er—it wasn't that, it was the way you cut through my politeness and told me what I really meant to say.'

'I have no time for beating about the bush, as the English call it.'

Taking that to heart, April reached to take the notebook from him, jumping slightly as her fingers accidentally brushed against his. It was as though she'd received an electric shock, and she blushed stupidly, fumbling to find the last few pages of shorthand.

She started reading aloud. Within seconds it became apparent that the Count's style of writing was as economical as his speech. There was no waffle, either in his style or coming from his characters. With nothing flowery about it, it was written in good, plain English, moving along at a steady pace so that April's interest was immediately caught and held.

The central character was a man named Sharkey. A ruthless man, who would do anything for money. At this point in the story he was in London, receiving a brief on a mission he was being asked to undertake in a tropical country on the African continent.

It was by no means the sort of stuff April usually read, but she knew she would enjoy it. What a nice way to earn a living, watching this intriguing story unfold!

'Are you ready, Miss Baxter?'

April picked up her pencil. 'Go ahead.'

The Count's chair tilted backwards as he leaned against it, hooking an ankle over his knee as he started dictating. '. . . Sharkey didn't hang around to hear the rest of it. He got abruptly to his feet and made for the door. 'Forget it,' he spat at Longman, 'the job's bloody impossible.' Longman surveyed him coolly. He wanted Sharkey for this job. Sharkey, and no one else. 'What would you say if I doubled your fee?' . . . At this, Sharkey turned from the door, his lips curling into a snarl. 'I'd say it's possible.' . . .'

For April it was a peculiar morning, a new way of working. The Count's dictation came in spasms, short and long. In the silences during which he was gathering his thoughts she didn't move a muscle, was afraid to distract him. By nine o'clock, she was more than ready for coffee.

The Count got up from his desk and moved around a bit, stretching his legs and moving in that stealthy, panther-like way of his. 'I've buzzed Finn. He'll bring coffee in a few minutes. How did it go?'

'The dictation? Fine.' April was bemused, wondering how he had managed to buzz Finn without her noticing. There must be a concealed button in his desk somewhere. How efficient this man was! How organised!

She glanced at her watch. 'Monsieur le Comte, I'd like to phone my agency, if I may. They'll be open now, and I'd better let them know where I am.' This was true enough, and she hadn't forgotten that she owed Phyllis a telling-off.

'By all means.' The Count moved over to his desk, picked up the silver cigarette box. 'There's a telephone in your office, which is right next door.' He nodded towards a communicating door in the corner of the room, which April hadn't even noticed. 'You can tell them off from me, too.'

'I beg your pardon?' She stopped in her tracks, frowning.

It was almost as if he thought she was playing a time-wasting game, the way he spelt out his next words. 'You came here on Saturday without the first clue as to what this job entailed. For starters, you hadn't even been told this was a living-in job. I heard the annoyance in your voice, Miss Baxter, and the way you so loyally tried to cover for your agency's lack of information. So, you're about to tell them off. Quite rightly.'

April left the room without saying anything. She sat by the telephone in her office but didn't pick it up straight away. Damn! How transparent she must have been at the interview! She knew that the remaining four senses of those who had lost their sight intensified, became far more efficient by way of compensation, but the Count could read every nuance, every inflection in speech, every sigh and smile!

Phyllis wasn't at the agency. It turned out that her weekend away was a long one, that she wouldn't be back till tomorrow. April sighed, put down the phone. Her anger had dissipated. After all, she'd got the job, was in Serena House and coping very well—so far.

There was no fire in her office, but there were two central heating radiators and it was warm, big and airy. The floor was covered in a thick wool carpet in a rust colour which was quite stimulating, giving the room an air of liveliness. There were three filing cabinets, a safe and, she was pleased to note, a golf ball typewriter with a self-corrector button. Next to that was a sheaf of typed papers—the earlier pages of chapter one of the Count's novel. Jason Jordan's novel. She looked forward to reading them, catching up with the story from the beginning.

When she went back into the library she was immediately struck by the aroma from the Count's cigarette. It was really quite pleasant. Obviously he smoked some foreign things—probably French.

The morning continued very satisfactorily, until April made her first mistake. When the Count called a halt she asked him where she might find the manuscripts of his last two books, saying she would like to read them.

In his smooth, velvet voice he answered pleasantly enough. 'They're in the top drawer of the filing cabinet. The one on the left. But ask Finn for copies of the printed versions, they'll be easier to handle.'

It was then that she dropped her clanger. 'Have you been writing long, Monsieur le Comte?'

A shadow crossed his face and the calmness she'd grown used to in his voice was suddenly absent. 'I was writing long before you had your first period pain.'

April's fingers curled tightly, her nails digging into the palms. What was *that* supposed to be—a test of her shockability? Well, she would not react. She absolutely would not give him the satisfaction of a reaction! She hadn't meant to refer to his past, she'd wondered only how long he had been writing as Jason Jordan.

One thing was certain: she would never, ever, again ask him anything which could be construed as even remotely personal.

CHAPTER FOUR

THE first few days at Serena House left April in a state of perplexity. Within le Comte Emile Jacquot de Nîmes were so many paradoxes. That he was a lonely man she was convinced. Yet he chose to live miles from anywhere, to guard his anonymity. He dressed in black, was always unsmiling, and wrote books which were riddled with violence. Yet he lived in a colourful, elegant house which was filled with beauty and romance in the form of art.

On the stair-wall and on the first floor landing, where her rooms were, April had seen two more Jacquot paintings. She remembered very clearly the contents of the drawing room, and dotted here and there—or rather, placed very carefully here and there—were precious and beautiful items. On the landing windowsill an exquisite porcelain vase, in the hall a magnificent twinkling chandelier, in the library, perched on a high, antique pedestal, a statue two feet high—a perfect nude made from bronze. There were so many things which were pleasing to the eye.

This—in the home of Jason Jordan?

This—in the home of a man who could not see?

For whose benefit were all these visual delights? To April's knowledge, in four days there had been no visitors, not even a phone call. Where was his wife? Had she perhaps gone to warmer climes for the winter? Maybe she was crazy enough to think she ought to leave him alone while he got on with his next book? But the Count said he lived alone—so maybe she had left altogether.

It would be perfectly reasonable to assume that the Count was nowadays a very different man from the one he used to be, when he was sighted. April found him difficult just to get on with; he was probably impossible actually to live with.

April got to her feet, moving around her sitting room restlessly. She needed a walk, a long, long walk. But it was bitterly cold outside. The snow was still heavy on the trees, still blanketing the ground, and underneath it was a layer of ice, encasing the earth and trying to prevent spring from coming. But it would not. Nature would catch up with herself. Spring was just around the corner.

She switched on the lamps and sat down again, enjoying her sitting room even as she felt the need to escape from it. Maybe it was just that she was lonely. Her evenings at Serena House were just as lonely as her evenings in London. But she had known that would be the case. At least it was no worse. And the view of the snow-clad grounds was far better than the view from her flat in Paddington.

It was quiet, too. She could hear no movement in the house—nothing at all. She found herself wondering what the Count was doing now. Taking a nap, perhaps? Listening to the radio? What did he do during the long hours he wasn't writing? Whatever— he was alone. And it seemed such a waste, such an awful waste.

She knew why he had given her the job, after rejecting four other people from Morrison's. Despite her clumsy reference to his past life, she had made adequate—more than adequate—compensation by showing him she was in no way inhibited by his blindness, or in the least embarrassed by it. The Count would not tolerate anyone who couldn't handle his handicap as well as he did. Between them, as far as this matter was concerned, there was a basic, unspoken understanding. But it wasn't enough for April. Why she felt such a need to communicate with her employer she couldn't say, except that she felt it would be as much for his good as for her own. Her attempts at conversation, however, during coffee breaks and before and after dictation, had been quelled with one of his short, dismissive sentences, leaving her in no doubt that he did not wish to establish any further understanding.

Finn knocked on her door a little after eight o'clock, and she gratefully accepted her dinner tray from him. Always there was a half bottle of wine on the tray. Sometimes April drank it, sometimes she didn't. It was always the correct wine for the food she was eating, and its presence made her smile. No doubt Finn did this as a matter of habit after tending to the Frenchman, for didn't the French always drink wine with their food?

'Your meals are always superb, Finn. Where did you learn to cook so well?' She gave him a bright smile as he set everything out on the table for her.

'Learn? I don't rightly remember. I suppose it comes naturally. Will you be taking coffee later, miss?'

'No, thanks. I'll come down and make myself some tea.'

'Very well. There's a laundry and dry-cleaning collection tomorrow. Is there anything you'd like to send?'

'No, thanks. Do you—do you have everything delivered to the house? I mean groceries and——'

'Yes, all the usual services, miss. I shall be driving into the village tomorrow, though. Is there something you wanted?'

'No, no, I just——' April sighed inwardly. Finn was so immaculate in his old-fashioned way but, like the Count, he had a superb knack of nipping conversation in the bud. Nonetheless, April took a chance and asked him a direct question. 'Why does the Count live in England? I—I remember reading somewhere that he's half English, in fact. But I seem to remember that the article said his home was in Paris?'

Finn's expression didn't change. 'I should have thought the answer's obvious, miss,' he said, as he moved towards the door. 'He must like it here. Goodnight, miss.'

April picked up her knife and fork, frowning. Had the inscrutable Finn been facetious just now? It was impossible to tell. But how could the Count like it here when he was a self-confessed hermit and couldn't even enjoy the view of the English countryside?

And what of Finn? What sort of life did he lead in his off-duty hours? Did he ever go out socially, or was he just as much a prisoner as his master? Finn gave nothing away. He was obviously very loyal and devoted to the man he'd known 'on and off' all his life—and was almost as much of a mystery. Finn would know the answers April was eager for, but there was no point in asking him anything personal, no point at all!

The evening was ahead of her, and April wondered what to do with it. For once she didn't feel like reading. Perhaps she'd have a long soak in the bath and then watch a little television. But first she would phone Alan. He was expecting her this weekend but didn't yet know that she would be working Saturday mornings and she wouldn't get to Surrey till the afternoon.

Alan greeted her warmly—a little too warmly. 'April! Thank goodness you've phoned. I've been trying to ring you this evening, but I couldn't get the number for a Mr Finn living at the address you showed me. Is it ex-directory or something?'

April laughed shortly. 'You might say that. But what's wrong? You could have phoned Morrison's to get this number.'

'I was going to, tomorrow. Anyway, nothing's wrong except that I'll have to put you off this weekend. We've all got stinking colds.'

April's heart sank. She'd thought her brother's voice sounded odd. 'Oh, well, you know I don't catch colds easily. I'll come just the same. I daresay you'll be glad of a hand if the kids are unwell.'

'Don't be daft. There's no point in taking a risk when you're in a new job, and the last thing you want is to end up with this lot.' He sneezed then, as if to prove his point.

'But you need help, Alan. I can at least cook——'

'No, I don't.' Her brother's voice was firm now. 'Liz's mother's coming tomorrow. She's staying for a few days. We'll be fine.'

'She's coming all the way from Taunton?' April tutted. Just as Liz had been, her mother was a very kind person. But she was no spring chicken and it was unfair to bring her all the way from Somerset to look after an ailing threesome.

'I know, I know.' Alan anticipated her next

question. 'I didn't send for her, if that's what you're thinking. She happened to phone earlier. Robert spoke to her first—and told her very gleefully that he hadn't been to school today. And why. After that, I couldn't keep her away.'

'Hm. Did you advertise for a housekeeper? I'm sure you lot don't eat properly. You've probably got colds because you're starved of the right vitamins.'

Alan laughed. 'It's possible. My advert was in the local paper Tuesday, yesterday and today, but so far, I haven't had a single phone call. Not one.'

'Then you'd better try the nationals.'

'That's expensive, Sis.'

'Alan . . .!'

'I'll do it! Give me your number so I can phone you next week.'

April gave him the number, and a warning never to ring before eleven in the morning.

After that she spent the rest of the evening in front of the telly. She would go home this weekend, but she was determined not to spend a day and a half with only the T.V., the washing machine and the vacuum cleaner for company. She'd got to the stage when she was starved for conversation. She would visit someone—or have a night out with Shirley, if she were available.

But April's weekend turned out to be horrid. Saturday night was not the best time to try and descend on people at such short notice. There was no reply from Shirley's number, one of her married friends had this wretched 'flu that was going around and another one had her in-laws staying for the weekend. So April had to make do with a solo visit to the cinema.

By the middle of the following week she was feeling much more cheerful. Alan had phoned to say everyone was practically recovered, the weather forecast promised warmer weather, and apart from all this she felt far more settled in her job.

Settled? She'd never felt unsettled. Anxious, yes, but not unsettled. Le Comte Emile Jacquot de Nîmes hadn't changed in any way. He was still as distant and uncommunicative as he'd been on the first day.

Nothing had changed. So why was she feeling so much happier? All things considered, the answer to that was strange, but April had to be honest with herself. She was happy because work was turning out to be such a pleasure. There was the unfolding story of Sharkey, Jason Jordan's hero, there was the sort of . . . emotional security . . . which one of her nature found in routine. But above all that, and despite his uncommunicativeness, there was the pleasure of being in the Count's company.

He fascinated her more and more with every passing day. She was able, now, to share his silence when he paused during dictation. His thoughts she could not share, of course, for the Count was concerned with Sharkey's next words, Sharkey's next deed, whereas April was concerned with the Count himself.

Again and again she had looked at Jacquot's painting over the fireplace and then looked at Jason Jordan. Not the Count, but Jason Jordan. How different Jacquot must have been! This man must have changed drastically. As drastically as his career had changed. He was still a creator, true. But April simply could not reconcile the romanticism, the sensitivity which had flowed from Jacquot with the rawness and violence which spewed from Jason Jordan.

Somewhere between the artist and the writer was the man himself. And it was he who fascinated her. He, the man who was today the sum total of all he had experienced, suffered, laughed at, feared and delighted in.

Emile Jacquot, the man.

On the Saturday of April's second week at Serena House the weather finally broke and she woke up to see a pale sun rising in a sky which promised to be blue. Tonight the clocks would go forward. Spring had arrived.

After experiencing the daily pleasure of first setting eyes on her employer, April bade him good morning as she took her seat beside his desk. Then, probably as a result of her high spirits, she ventured a comment about the weather. 'We've seen the last of the snow.' She smiled, knowing he would hear that smile. 'And pretty though it was, I resent it for having kept me indoors so much. But it's going now.' She looked beyond him, to the gardens outside the library. 'And the trees are melting.'

Emile Jacquot leaned back in his chair, his fingers strumming lightly against the arm. 'You mean the thaw has set in.'

It wasn't a question, for he probably knew full well what the weather was doing. It was one of his conversation-stoppers.

'All right, if that's how you'd rather put it.'

The beautifully sculptured face turned towards her, his coal black eyes locking on to hers in that uncanny way of his. 'But aren't you the girl who told me she's a realist? Miss Baxter, realists don't talk in terms of trees melting.'

April was momentarily stumped. He was right, of

course. But what was this—conversation? Or was it politeness because he'd heard a hint of irritation in her voice? No, this wasn't just politeness, because he was looking at her expectantly now, as if he wanted a reply. Then he was smiling at her and she giggled because it pleased her so much. Just a smile. How easy it should be to smile, but she could count on one hand the number of times he had treated her to one over the past fourteen days.

Clearly the Count was in a good mood this morning, and April didn't hesitate to plunge right in while the going was good. 'Monsieur le Comte, there's something I wanted to ask you today. I'm going to see my brother this afternoon and—well, he'll be naturally curious as to who it is I'm working for. He—he knows you're a writer, but . . . I mean, may I tell him who you are?'

There was a brief bow of the head as permission was granted and his smile grew even broader. 'Of course you may. I'm sure your brother is discreet. I don't think for one minute that he's likely to place an advertisement in *The Times*.'

April was almost lightheaded, enjoying herself. 'No—not about this matter, anyway!'

'*Pardon?*'

'Sorry. Forget it.' The Count's remark had reminded her of Alan's housekeeper problem.

His dark eyebrows rose slightly. 'What have I hit upon? Your brother works for a national newspaper, is that it?'

'No. Alan's a solicitor. It—it was only that you reminded me of something else. He was supposed to put in an advert for a housekeeper this week. He's so badly in need of someone. In fact, I'm so anxious about him that I nearly didn't come here for the interview! I wanted—I mean—no, that's not true. Alan wouldn't . . .'

No longer pleased with herself, April's voice faded. Now she was actually talking with the Count, she had become tongue-tied, nervous. Besides, this wasn't really conversation, she was just waffling, and he couldn't possibly be interested.

But he was. 'Explain,' said the brown velvet voice.

It was nice, the way he got her to talk then. Clever, too. He didn't urge her to go on, he just leaned forward, his arms on the desk and his hands held loosely together. Just as it had been when he was drawing her out at the interview, his head was slightly inclined in an attitude of listening, and on his face was that look of concentration which told April she had his undivided attention.

She told him about Alan and his children. How they'd recently been unwell, how they needed someone to look after them, how she'd volunteered to do the job herself. And how Alan had refused. At this point she was so relaxed and natural that she didn't think about her final comment. 'So I told Alan he was potty, that I'd end up a maiden aunt in any case. But I couldn't change his mind. He insisted I had my own life to lead, and that was that.'

A few seconds passed before the Count commented, 'He's absolutely right. You must lead your own life. Alan sounds like a good man. Tell me about him.'

There was silence. April was baffled. She should have known the Count wasn't merely being polite, that wasn't his style. He was genuinely interested in her family, but she couldn't imagine why.

'April?' Then, 'I may call you April?'

'Of—of course.'

'And do you think you could manage to address me with a little less formality?'

A little less formality? She did it correctly, taking his surname, just as Finn did when he was addressing the Count directly. 'Yes, Monsieur Jacquot.'

He grinned, leaning forward and speaking to her as if she were retarded. 'Try this . . . E-m-i-l-e.'

April's eyebrows went up in astonishment. She parroted the name exactly as he had said it.

'Well done! Now—you were going to tell me about your brother.'

'Y-yes. But he—Alan's so ordinary, you see. So ordinary that it's hard to describe him really.'

She started doodling on her notebook, her lower lip caught between her teeth as she thought how best to describe her brother. 'Let me put it this way, if Alan were—er—let's say if he were a building, for example, he'd be the Town Hall, because that's practical, functional, if you see what I mean. And if he were a colour, he'd be khaki, a sensible colour, warmish but rather dull.'

'I get the idea—the feeling.' The Count didn't laugh at her, on the contrary, he entered into the spirit of the thing. 'And if he were a glass, he'd be an ordinary pint pot, *n'est-ce pas?*'

'Quite so!' she laughed.

'And if he were water, what form would he take?'

'Ah! That's a good one!' She beamed at him. 'A good question, that, because water takes so many shapes, has so many moods. So, Alan would be . . . yes, he'd be a pond—large and still, and, I'm sorry to say, just a little bit stagnant.'

The Count nodded slowly, interestedly. 'Now tell me, April, if you were water, what would *you* be?'

She thought hard about that, pleased that he was interested but obliged to tell the truth. 'The same, I'm afraid.'

'Wrong!' Now his smile was a sudden flash of white that made her heartbeat accelerate suddenly. At that instant, his eyes appeared to be different again. They seemed to be dark brown, warm and full of humour.

'All right,' she challenged, 'then you tell me what I'd be.'

But the Count suddenly withdrew. 'Some other time,' he said dismissively. 'We must press on with our work now.'

It was as if he'd had enough of frivolity—or suddenly realised she was wasting his time. Either way, the mood, the atmosphere changed so abruptly that it left April feeling disproportionately, ridiculously upset.

When the writing session ended, a little before eleven, she got to her feet and told him she was leaving straight away for Surrey. 'I'll type today's work tomorrow evening, when I get back.'

The Count nodded, making no comment, and April left the room as he swung his chair round to face the window. No doubt the sun was quite high by now, but he could feel through the window nothing of its warmth. And what of the snow? Had it vanished completely—or were the trees still melting?

She was nice to have around, this girl who brought an essence of roses into the room each morning. He couldn't place her perfume. Probably it was English, since it had a typically English fragrance.

Wryly, Emile Jacquot smiled to himself. Ah, but

he'd been unable to resist today! How could she possibly think herself a realist when so often the things she said were phrased so poetically? And her voice, that soft, ultra-feminine voice with its shy giggle and throaty laugh—how often it held a note of surprise! She took such delight in simple things. He could hear again the touching enthusiasm when she had told him, one morning earlier in the week, that a magpie had just come to rest outside the window. Then, as if it were vitally important, she'd added, 'Oh, his mate has come along! Thank goodness—because when you see magpies, it's "one for sorrow, two for joy", you know!'

He had said nothing. He hadn't known quite how to respond, had almost forgotten what it was like to talk at this level, to enthuse over birds playing in the garden. But there had been a time when he'd have— no, he *must not* look back. There was discipline in his life now, a strict discipline without which he could not function. In his movements, his routine, there were limitations which had been forced upon him. But they were easy enough to live with. That which had taken time, that which had required the main adjustment, was the training of his mind—the emotional cut-out. But he'd succeeded, eventually. His mind, now, ran along limited grooves which permitted no meandering, no sentimentality.

That April Baxter was deeply intuitive and sensitive he had realised by the way she had brought the interview to a close; indeed she had behaved as if she had read his very thoughts. But he had not realised she was such a romantic. He had not realised she would be such a breath of fresh air—a delight which he could not afford to respond to.

He had responded today, had felt a need to get

closer to her. But it would not happen again. It *must* not happen again. It was too dangerous, far too dangerous. He dared not risk any disturbance, any resurrection of the kind of emotions and thoughts it had taken him five years to combat, to bury.

No, he simply dared not allow himself to drink of the sweet and sparkling fountain that was April.

CHAPTER FIVE

'WELL?' April looked expectantly at her brother. 'What do you make of the Count, from what I've told you?'

Alan Baxter was puffing away at his pipe, surprised by the intensity in his sister's voice. He shrugged. 'He's nothing like the mental picture I'd drawn of Jason Jordan. But it's good, eh, working for such a well-known novelist? I really enjoy his books!'

April's disappointment was equal to the annoyance she felt with herself. She had hoped Alan would understand why she was so intrigued, but she should have known he wouldn't. She'd by no means given Alan all her impressions concerning the Count, but she had told him enough that he might form an opinion.

Alan's reaction, on hearing of the Count's other identities, had been quite the reverse of April's. He had been tremendously impressed, almost excited, to learn that his sister was working for Jason Jordan— and barely interested at all that that same man was also Jacquot, the artist whose work would have brought such pleasure to the masses if only——

But that was Alan. 'Why have you gone quiet?' he teased then, 'you've only been talking about the man for an hour—but don't let that stop you!'

April smiled. Had she really gone on for an hour? Alan was probably bored rigid by now. 'Sorry. Shall I start dinner? It'll take some time. When will the

73

children be back from their party?'

'Don't worry about that. They won't want dinner after they've been stuffing themselves with cake and ice-cream all afternoon.' He paused, considering. 'But go on, April. What was it you were asking me? I mean, what did you want me to say about this Jordan chap?'

There was no point in pursuing this conversation. She had wanted Alan's opinion of the Count, his impressions from what she had told him about the contradictory elements.

'Oh, nothing. It—I was only wondering if you agreed with me that he's a lonely man.'

'I daresay he is,' said Alan, tapping his pipe noisily against an ashtray. 'But as you said, he chooses to live miles from anywhere, not to have visitors and so on. But why should you be so bothered, anyway? You're not falling for him, are you?'

For one who intended to let the conversation fizzle out, April responded violently to that. 'Don't be ridiculous! He's a married man! Besides, you don't think a man like him would be interested in a girl like me!'

'I don't see why not. April, why is it you always put yourself down whenever we broach the subject of men, your attractiveness, your femininity?'

'Come on, Alan. You're my brother, so I expect honesty. Let's face it, I'm not exactly a looker!'

He was filling his pipe again, and his prolonged preoccupation with it was beginning to annoy her. 'But the Count doesn't know that.'

'Alan . . .?'

'No, I didn't mean that in any nasty way, and you know it. All I'm saying is that men aren't always attracted to women because of their looks. And you know that, too. What about your lovely personality? What about your sincerity, your intelligence, your patience?'

Patience. She was fast losing that right now. 'You're my brother—you're bound to think I have those qualities. You're biased.'

'Rubbish! Because I'm your brother I can be more objective. So while we're on the subject, let me put you straight on something else. You are *not* un-attractive. You're average-looking, true. And lately you're getting a little heavy on the hips, but you don't exactly doll up and make the most of yourself, do you? I mean, if you did something with your hair and put on some make-up, you'd be able to attract lots of men who——'

'Who'd later discover what a lovely person I am,' she finished.

'I wasn't going to say that. Not quite that, anyway.'

'Then you were about to give me the "you're almost twenty-four and it's high time you got married" lecture.' April got to her feet, helped herself to a cigarette from the box on the mantelpiece. This conversation was suddenly very irritating.

Alan didn't seem to notice her irritation. Just now he appeared to be preoccupied with something other than his pipe. 'Oh, yes,' he said slowly, as if he'd just solved a problem, 'I remember where I saw it now . . .'

April said nothing. She lit her cigarette and thought that the sooner this conversation was dropped, the better.

'. . . Emile Jacquot isn't married, actually. He got divorced some time ago . . . I remember reading about it.'

The heavy onyx table lighter was still in April's hand. Her fingers involuntarily tightened against it as she made an effort to keep her voice even, nonchalant. 'Are you sure?'

Her brother looked almost offended. 'You know I've got a very retentive memory, of course I'm sure! I read about it, I tell you. I'd just been trying to remember where. Mmm, that's right—Jacquot was married to a Françoise something or other, and she took up with another man, someone in films . . . I say, she was a very beautiful woman, wasn't she, his wife? I remember the photo . . .'

April looked down at the object in her hands, weighing it as if it would help her to weigh up her reaction to this news.

She looked up to find Alan watching her, frowning with unmistakable disapproval. 'Sis, you are falling for this man, aren't you?'

'Alan, if you say that again I shall leave, and you can cook your own flaming dinner!'

'I haven't seen you so—so strung-up—in a long time. Well, if you'll take my advice you'll stop this thing before it starts. You should leave that house straight——'

'What the devil are you talking about?' She was on her feet again, disturbed, disturbed, disturbed. Stop it before it starts? What was there to stop? And leave Serena House? How could she possibly do that, even if she wanted to——

But the thought did not develop any further, because Alan's next remark tipped the balance and she lost her temper completely.

'I mean, you don't want to risk getting involved with a blind man, do you?'

April Baxter, normally so slow to anger, almost jumped down his throat. '*What?* What the hell has his eyesight got to do with anything?'

Alan didn't even have the good grace to look ashamed. He just stuck his pipe between his teeth and spoke to her as if she were ten years old and he was Methuselah. 'Now you're being silly. You know the answer to that just as well as I. What sort of life would it be for you—with a blind man? You want to nip it in the bud. I mean, why him? Even if he is Jason Jordan! Why go for a man who can't——'

'Stop it!' She ground her cigarette into the ashtray, marched across the room and flung open the door. 'I'm going to start dinner. I'm sorry, Alan, but I want no more discussion on this. Not now. Not ever. You just don't know what you're talking about. Besides,' she flung over her shoulder, 'it's a purely hypothetical conversation in any case.'

But she simply could not let it go at that, hypothetical or not, and she quickly backtracked to the living room doorway. 'I find your comments about Emile's handicap disgusting! Worse than that, they frighten me, because I wonder by what yardstick you measure a man's worth!'

She was still upset when Alan ventured into the kitchen half an hour later. But she smiled at him— because he was her brother and one loves one's brother regardless. They were close, they'd always been close, but April had long since realised that their thinking was quite, quite different. There were depths to which Alan could not go, things about human nature which he would probably never understand.

He slipped an arm around her. 'Sorry. I can't help being your big brother, you know.'

'I know, and it's all right.' Big brother? There were times when she felt years older than he was.

'Hey, you haven't heard my news! About the housekeeper.'

April felt instantly guilty. She'd done so much talking since she'd arrived—and this matter she had clean forgotten about. 'You've found someone?'

'Not exactly, but I'm optimistic. I put an ad in the *Telegraph*—just for one issue—and I've had five phone calls. But there's one woman who sounds particularly promising. She's Scottish, coming down to see me next week. 'Course, I'll have to pay her expenses, but she sounded ever so nice on the phone. She's been a housekeeper for years, working in a huge house for Sir somebody or other. I've got it all written down, and I'm going to write for a reference. The chap she was working for died, you see, so she's redundant. But she's told me I can get a reference from the chap's daughter.'

April's eyebrows rose slightly. 'Did you tell her this is only a four-bedroomed house—but there are two children to care for?'

'Of course.'

But of course he had. Alan would have explained everything meticulously, nothing understated, nothing exaggerated. Good old Alan. Sensible Alan. He was sweet, in his own way, but oh, there were times when he could be incredibly insensitive!

April left her brother's house on the following afternoon, went home to pick up some more clothes and then, on an impulse, she went to Shirley's place before heading back to Serena House. She was still keen to get another point of view as far as the Count was concerned—and Shirley's opinion was one she would value. April knew she could speak to Shirley in confidence, and it would be interesting to hear another woman's impressions.

Shirley flung open the door of her flat wearing rubber gloves, a stained overall—and a big grin. 'Hi! Come in, April, come in! Long time, no see! I've been so busy—Glad you're here, it'll give me the perfect excuse to stop cleaning!'

'I did phone you last weekend, several times, actually.' April followed her friend into the tiny kitchen and sat herself at the little breakfast bar.

Shirley was already filling the kettle and getting out coffee cups. 'Ah, well, I have news for you! I was in Leeds last weekend and I'll be there next weekend, too. Hold on to your hat, kiddo, Paul and I are moving to Leeds after we get married! He's been offered a job at Head Office—a desk job! Isn't that great? It means he'll do hardly any travelling now, he'll be coming home to me every night.' She was freeing her dark hair from the ponytail clip which had been keeping it off her face, and still grinning like a Cheshire cat.

'Well, that is good news!' April smiled. 'Except that I'll be sorry to lose you to the North Country. I'll miss you. So you'll be making several trips up there till you find yourselves a house, is that it?'

'Yep! Oh—do you fancy a sandwich?'

'No, thanks. And you'll be moving immediately after the wedding, at the end of July?'

The following half hour was spent with Shirley talking about her plans, the wedding reception, wedding rings and the type of outfit April would buy for the big day. It was Shirley herself who finally changed the subject, realising she'd gone on quite enough about her own news and had hardly given April a chance to speak.

'Sorry, April—you've hardly got a word in.' Shirley leaned over and patted the other girl fondly. 'I've missed seeing you these last few weeks, that's the trouble. I know I've been a stick-in-the-mud, not coming out, but we're trying to save every penny——'

'That's all right—I understand.'

'Tell me your news, then. I hear you're working for Jason Jordan! Exciting, eh? I also hear that he's a bit of a weirdo!' She looked at April expectantly.

April was not at all surprised that the agency grapevine had reached Shirley; that was nothing unusual. But the offensive description of Jason Jordan disturbed her. It was so unlike Shirley. In fact ... April's eyes narrowed thoughtfully. 'Who've you been talking to? Has Phyllis told you this?'

'No, I——' Shirley paused, a little nonplussed by April's tone. 'I've been working with Greg Stanton this week, and he'd been for an interview with Mr Jordan.'

April sighed, understanding at last. Greg Stanton. He'd joined Morrison's about six months earlier and was probably their fastest shorthand writer. He was also very charming, but there was no depth to the man. None at all. April had had one, and only one, date with him some time ago—and had been bored rigid all evening.

'For all his surface charm,' she told Shirley, 'Greg Stanton is actually the most cynical man I've met. He wouldn't begin to understand a man like Jason Jordan, and that remark is just typical of him. I can't imagine why Phyllis sent him for an interview!'

'I wouldn't know about that. It seems that several

people were sent for interviews. Anyway, Greg asked Phyllis who it was that finally landed the job, and she said you'd started work for Mr Jordan a couple of weeks ago. Er . . . Greg also told me that Mr Jordan is blind. Is that right?' Shirley looked almost apologetic, realising she'd been misled by Greg Stanton to some extent, and seeking to make amends.

'That much is true, but there's nothing weird about him, I can assure you. He—he is something of a mystery, though . . .' She paused. 'Have you heard anything else about him?'

'No. Not a thing.'

So none of the other interviewees had recognised Jason Jordan as Jacquot . . . 'Listen, Shirley, I don't want this to go any further, but Jason Jordan is—was—known by another name.'

'So Jason Jordan is his pen-name, I gathered that much.'

'No—I mean yes. He's—I don't know whether this will mean anything to you, but he's also Emile Jacquot. Jacquot was a famous——'

'Painter!' Shirley's eyebrows went up in surprise. 'The one who lost his sight! Yes, of course I know of him. Why, you've got a painting of his, haven't you?'

'A reproduction,' April corrected. 'Mmm. Actually, his full name is Le Comte Emile Jacquot de Nîmes . . .'

Shirley listened in fascination as April went on to tell her about the Count, about his life-style and the mystery surrounding it. 'Anyway,' she said at length, 'I can't weigh him up. Have you got any ideas?'

Shirley was quiet for a moment, thinking about it. 'There's got to be a woman involved somewhere. Is he married, or what?'

'*Cherchez la femme,*' April smiled. 'I'd had a similar thought, but he's divorced, actually. Alan told me yesterday. It seems his wife went off with an actor, or something. It was all reported in the papers.'

'I see. That sounds a bit odd, doesn't it? I mean, the Count being so good-looking and all, with everything he has going for him.' Shirley's face was sombre and April could see her mulling it all over in her mind, just as she'd done herself.

'I can quite see why you're fascinated by Emile,' Shirley said at length. 'Its odd the way he's cut himself off from life, I mean, it isn't as if his blindness is a great problem to him. From what you've told me, he handles that very well . . . I wonder . . .'

'Yes?'

'. . . If perhaps he's still in love with his wife? Missing her?'

'Françoise? No, I don't think—well, I suppose it's possible.'

'Very possible.' Shirley said firmly. 'It makes sense to me. Makes sense of the way he is now, I mean. Shall we have some more coffee?'

'No, thanks. I'd better push off, I don't want to drive back in the dark—there's a danger I'd get lost! Look, I'll give you my phone number, but please don't ring before eleven o'clock.'

Shirley made a note of the number at Serena House and promised to keep in touch. 'I'll be interested to see what else you find out about this Emile Jacquot! And don't worry—it'll go no further, you know that.'

There was this lovely feeling of coming home. The Alsatians were there, barking their heads off, their teeth bared and terrifying. There was Finn's gruff voice over the intercom, checking lest it was someone other than April who had the audacity to attempt penetration of the Count's private world.

But in spite of the welcoming committee, April knew that warm feeling one experiences on arriving home. She loved Serena House. Within its walls she found tranquillity, beauty, an atmosphere which could be likened to nowhere else.

It was strange she should feel these things when the main occupant of the house was an incredibly unhappy man. Strange that she couldn't wait to get back to the place whenever she left it, when she herself knew many hours of loneliness here. Strange indeed that this place had become home to her, far more than Alan's house or even her own flat.

After thinking about it on the way home, April had dismissed Shirley's idea. Emile still in love with his ex-wife? No, that didn't sound at all right.

As for Alan—well, she was disgusted at his reaction, and that particular discussion had left her feeling distinctly twitchy. In time, she would solve the mystery of Emile Jacquot for herself. She was determined to do that. But she didn't stop to ask herself why she was so determined, why she was so interested.

In the meantime there was work to do and the bloody adventures of Sharkey would provide a complete distraction. April put her car in the big garage and got down to work straight away.

When she got to the first floor landing, her typing finished, she saw the Count disappearing through a door at the far end of the corridor. His rooms overlooked the front of the house, while April's were at the rear. He stopped, turned, hearing her footsteps despite the fact that they were made inaudible by the plush carpet.

He said, 'Good evening, April.' And then he was gone.

He didn't ask how she was, what sort of weekend she'd had, whether she'd got up to date with her work—nothing. April flopped down tiredly on the lilac bedspread. In her mind she was back in the library, reliving Saturday's conversation and enjoying again his enjoyment at the silly way she'd tried to describe Alan. Emile had understood her instantly, got the feeling—as he'd put it—of what she was trying to convey. But that had been their only conversation to date, and how frustrating it was that he had withdrawn again.

And his withdrawal continued. It was almost as if that conversation had been some sort of aberration on his part. April was appalled, but what could she say? He was the boss, and he continued daily to speak out the pages of his book, and that was all.

But she was damned if he'd make her as withdrawn as he was! So she told him, when she felt like it, of the little pleasing things she had seen happening during her walks in the grounds, like the crocuses peeping from the earth or the daffodils' valiant attempts at survival after last month's snow. Or she'd tell him she'd been window-shopping in Leighton Buzzard, attended a poetry-reading circle which she'd discovered in Bletchley, or of the books she'd read, borrowed from his fabulous library. Of course, she got hardly any response, but she chatted through their coffee-breaks regardless, determined not to be put off by his attitude, determined to continue to be herself.

About a month after April had moved into Serena

House there was a brief, off-duty encounter which left
her realising that she had in fact been communicating
with the Count all along, albeit in a small way. It was
around nine o'clock, one evening when she strolled out
into the garden. The black sky was studded with stars
and a stark silver moon which was full. She caught the
aroma of Emile's cigarette before her eyes came to rest
on his dark outline. His long legs were stretched out
before him, one hand thrust inside the pocket of his
slacks, and he sat, unmoving, lost in his thoughts.

April had found him like this before, in the library
at the break of day. Many times she had found him
thinking, staring into the distance, into the blackness
which was perpetually his. She knew at those times he
was not thinking about his book because his eyes
would be bleak, grey, and long seconds would pass
before he acknowledged her presence.

It was like that now. She sat beside him, silent,
sensing, even feeling, his sadness, and bided her time
before she spoke. 'The sky is very beautiful tonight.'

For a while he didn't speak, didn't move. Then he
turned to her. 'Is it, April?' Then, in a very quiet
voice, 'Paint it for me, April. Paint it in words.'

In words . . .? She felt a sort of panic because she
was almost desperate not to let him down, but unsure
what he expected of her.

'Go on, April. Don't think about it, don't try to
choose your words, just talk. You have the most
delightful way of describing things, do you know that?
It's a gift. You should try writing yourself. I mean it.
Please, paint the scene for me now.'

She did. It just flowed from her, easily, un-
selfconsciously. She painted everything, even the
things he knew about, like the stillness, the silence.

She described the trees, the shadows they cast, the moon, the stars, the outline of the house and all the light and form she could see, shimmering or unmoving.

In those few minutes April felt incredibly, joyously happy. How wonderful to be able to give pleasure so simply. How wonderful that he'd asked her to!

She could have gone on for ever. She wanted to walk with him around the entire grounds, around the house, the world, and describe to him everything she saw.

But the moment was quickly over. Abruptly he got to his feet and moved away from her. 'Please excuse me now.'

'Emile . . .?'

'I must think about tomorrow's work. Goodnight.'

It was like a slap in the face, and foolish tears welled up in April's eyes. She watched him as he walked away, his sadness draped around him like a cloak. It had been a beautiful exchange, and that part of him which was Jacquot must surely mourn for moments like——

As the realisation struck her she buried her face in hands which had grown cold.

Emile Jacquot *was* a man in mourning.

A small cry escaped from her as everything, but *everything* started falling into place, and she suddenly found herself face to face with the core of Emile Jacquot.

She thought of the paradoxes in his lifestyle, the house filled with art and colour. She had a mental picture of him moving around the library during dictation—the way his hands would trail lovingly along the sculptures in there . . .

He was mourning for his art. His *true* art. That which he would never again be able to create for as long as he lived. Witness this house, the beauty of it, the paintings—*his* paintings. There lay the answer to this dichotomy in his nature. In every other respect Emile had put the past behind him. He had cut everyone and everything from his life. Except art. Except beauty. Those things he could not bear to part with, he could not live without.

He knew every inch of the house? Indeed he did. He could see the beauty surrounding him just as clearly as April. Better, even!

In the dead of night April was still thinking about him. Tears streamed down her face. Tears not for Emile, but for herself. She could hear Alan's words, Alan's *accusation* echoing round her head . . . 'You are falling for this man, aren't you?' . . . and her mind screamed out the admission. Yes, I am. I am! And I don't give a damn! It could bring only heartache, she knew that, because Emile Jacquot would never feel anything for her.

She'd known this would happen. Right from the start she'd known it . . . that feeling of excitement tinged with uneasiness.

She smiled sadly, flicking back through the entries in her diary. Such euphemisms, such rationalisations she'd used over the weeks in an effort to disguise her real feelings for Emile! What a stupid thing to do, trying to fool herself like that. Why hadn't she admitted that she'd started to love him from the beginning—and it scared the hell out of her?

That she would love Emile had been inevitable, unavoidable—as was the pain which came with that love. The two were inseparable because she knew her love was impotent, futile, destined to burn for a man who would never feel its warmth.

The coldness, the desolation and unhappiness which formed the central core of Emile Jacquot, was untouchable. It was as if April had seen the sought-after centre of a maze even while she stood on the outside of it. There were so many paths, so many layers protecting that centre. His apparent warmth, the sensitivity and humour were not real, they were merely layers beyond layers. He had allowed her to glimpse some of them because she'd tried so hard for the privilege. But they no longer deceived her. Beyond them was a man who had simply given up on life, a man who cared for nothing. Oh, he was still functioning, going through the motions, but the heart of the man had frozen solid five years ago.

How could a girl such as she ever hope to melt that heart—even if she were able to find a path which would lead to it?

She couldn't.

It was true that during the occasions when they'd talked there was a tremendous rapport, a deep intuitive understanding of one another. But then he would withdraw so completely, so sharply it was almost as if he felt he'd let himself down in some way. He didn't *want* people. Witness his lifestyle, his withdrawal from the world. Emile Jacquot simply didn't *need* people.

He had lost his sight, his ability to paint, and now he was in mourning. And she'd been foolish enough to think he'd adjusted! Nothing and nobody could console that sort of grief. No wonder there were times when she could feel his sadness as if it were tangible.

April looked down at her diary. She simply couldn't

commit all these thoughts to paper. There would be such a dreadful finality in writing it down. Besides, what she felt for Emile was too vulnerable, too precious to be put into words which would probably prove inadequate. So she would leave on the page just one sentence. It would risk no distortion of the emotion, the pain and the hopelessness if she kept to her own private code and wrote, simply, 'Colour me blue.'

CHAPTER SIX

DURING the following days April had to make a tremendous effort to be herself, to appear unchanged in any way. It wasn't easy, and the strain took its toll. One morning she woke up with a screaming headache, a sense of panic rising in her throat. She looked at her clock. Four-thirty. Again she'd slept badly, for barely three hours, but she might just as well get up. There would be no peaceful sleep for her until she came to terms with the futility of loving Emile Jacquot. That, she had to do, otherwise the remaining months at Serena House would become unbearable.

She pulled on a pair of slacks and a heavy sweater, dragged a comb through her hair and climbed into her boots. Very quietly she went downstairs and headed for the back door. But she needn't have bothered pussyfooting; Finn was already in the kitchen, which meant the Count was up, too.

''Morning, Finn.' She was deliberately short with him because for the first time ever she had caught an expression on his face—one of near-embarrassment.

He was sitting at the kitchen table, drinking tea and reading, wearing horrible navy blue striped pyjamas and a brown dressing-gown. April tried to spare him unnecessary embarrassment by walking straight out the kitchen door, for he had got to his feet when she appeared, quickly, as if she'd caught him doing something wicked.

She walked and walked, farther than she'd walked before, until she reached the woods at the end of the grounds. It didn't do her much good, the tension inside her negated any benefit she might have got from the crisp morning air and the exercise. In the semi-darkness she picked wild flowers from the edge of the wood, an armful of them, and headed back to the house when the throbbing in her temples got to the pitch when she could stand it no longer.

Coming up the smooth lawn at the back of the house she saw the lights were on in the pool room. She'd seen the swimming pool many times before, of course, it was built into an extension which had been very thoughtfully designed to blend in with the appearance of the main building. But she'd never seen anyone actually using it before.

The Count was in there now, cutting through the water at a terrific pace as he swam length after length. April stood and watched. She was near enough to see him through the tall sliding doors which would open on to the lawn in the summer months, but sufficiently distant so that even he, with his inbuilt radar, wouldn't sense her presence.

When he got out of the water, she gulped, feeling guilty at her accidental invasion of his privacy. He was naked.

She should have moved then, should have got quickly out of sight in case Finn spotted her from the kitchen window. But she didn't. Nor did she feel any embarrassment. Watching him stand by the pool, raking the dark hair away from his face, she knew only a sense of awe at his sheer, masculine beauty. Deliberately, as if she were viewing a work of art, she drank in the sight of his tall and powerful body. It was a pleasure she unashamedly allowed herself for two or three precious minutes.

Finn was taking plates out of the dishwasher. He was dressed now, clean shaven and recognisable. 'Good morning again, Miss Baxter. You're up very early today.'

April thought she saw, but couldn't be certain because it would be a lot to ask, a look of approval in his watery eyes. 'Yes. Finn, could you find me a vase for these flowers, and a couple of Aspirins?'

He nodded, and April laid the flowers on the draining board and switched the kettle on.

'I'll make your tea and toast, miss.' Finn handed her a large crystal vase and a bottle of Aspirins.

'No toast today, thanks. Just tea. And I'll have it in here.'

'Interesting about the Aspirins,' said Finn, 'I've heard it said that if you put a couple in the water it helps the flowers to live longer.'

At any other time April would have laughed, at his unintended joke and because he was actually volunteering conversation. But laughter was beyond her this morning, and she simply put him straight as to why she had asked for the tablets.

Finn's way of being sympathetic was to grunt. 'So that's why you went out so early.'

April sighed. 'I couldn't sleep. Do you always get up in the middle of the night?'

'No, miss. Half past four every day. Monsieur Jacquot takes coffee in the poolroom at five, then he has his swim, and he likes a cooked breakfast at six. If you'll excuse me, I must get on with his breakfast now.'

April took her flowers upstairs and had a shower.

She must try to pull herself together. She didn't want to appear different in any way at all.

The Aspirins didn't help much, though. By eight-thirty her headache was back with a vengeance and she was having difficulty focusing on her notebook. When Finn came in with coffee she smiled up at him gratefully. He had put a couple of tablets on the tray for her. How clever of him, she thought, surprised. She didn't want Emile to know something was wrong, and now he wouldn't need to. Finn gave her one of his brief nods, but the florid, inscrutable face didn't grant her as much as a smile.

But Emile Jacquot didn't need to see tablets to know something was wrong. He had sensed the tension in April from the moment she had walked into the room, and now he was missing her delightful coffee-time chatter. In fact, she hadn't been herself for several days.

'What's wrong, April?' The concern in the deep voice startled her.

'Wrong? Nothing's wrong.'

'April . . .' It sounded like a warning.

'Oh, I'm just a little short of sleep, I suppose. Must have a nap this afternoon.'

'How bad is it?'

'How bad is what?'

'Your headache, you wretched girl! How bad is your headache?'

She laughed. Because at times he appeared to be almost psychic, because he was telling her not to beat about the bush, and because it served as a small release of the tension inside her, she laughed. 'Emile, I'm perfectly well. Please don't fuss.'

His tongue made a clicking sound and he just left

her to stew in silence until she gave in.

'All right, all right! It's chronic.'

Emile nodded, satisfied. 'Finish your coffee, then off you go.'

'Eh?'

'Eh?' he mocked. 'To bed. Off you go to bed.'

'Certainly not! We've got a schedule to keep. Besides, we can't leave Sharkey bleeding to death in the middle of a tropical jungle!'

Emile threw back his head and laughed. This girl was irrepressible, damn her! Damn her for her kindness, her constancy, her femininity, for making him feel alive for four hours every day . . .

'*Ça va sans dire*, Avril. Sharkey will live, you know that. He must live to tell the tale—and to fight another day. Now stop trying to distract me! Go and lie down.'

Reluctantly, gratefully, she left him. Against the morning light she drew her curtains and lay on top of the bed . . . and within minutes she found herself weeping.

She didn't fight it, she just cried until there were no more tears. It helped, she'd known it would, this release of emotion.

Physically she was far worse off. Her temples were pounding and her hands trembling as she picked up the phone and told Finn she wouldn't be having lunch today.

Finn went as far as offering a protest, suggesting that food might be a cure-all. April thanked him, overrode his protest.

In the kitchen of Serena House there was a momentary stillness as Finn looked thoughtfully at the telephone receiver. She'd sounded very odd . . .

'All right, Finn. Thank you. You did right to tell me. Would you pour me a brandy, since you're here?'

The Count was sitting in the overstuffed armchair by the fire in the drawing room.

Finn looked nonplussed. Brandy? At this hour? It seemed that the day's routine was being broken in more ways than one ... 'I—didn't want to trouble you, Monsieur Jacquot. It's just that Miss Baxter looked very pale this morning. I mean, she's always pale, but—well, I thought she might be sickening for something. That is to say—er—she's normally such a pleasant, cheerful sort of girl and——'

'Yes, Finn. You carry on with lunch as usual. Miss Baxter will be eating. She'll take lunch with me today.'

His old and trusty servant nearly dropped the brandy decanter. 'I'm sorry, what did you say?'

'I said Miss Baxter will be lunching with me today.'

'With you, sir? You mean—in the dining room with you?'

Emile laughed shortly, hollowly. 'Where else? Make that two brandies will you? Just put them here on the table.'

Finn said nothing more. He did as he was bade and left the room, thoroughly confused.

Emile lit a cigarette, battling with himself. He would have to go to her. He was at least partly responsible for her tension, of that he was sure. She was a sensitive creature and he'd treated her shabbily. You couldn't do that to a girl like April and expect it to have no effect.

Hell, why did she have to be so intuitive, so responsive? Why couldn't she be like his other secretaries and natter about the price of food, or clothes—or just ignore him? She was too wise for her years. Too perceptive. She was altogether unsuitable.

He should never have hired her in the first place.

Even his writing was being affected. Never before had he made so many alterations to a manuscript—and that in itself was giving April more pressure. She never complained. Always she'd say something encouraging, 'Oh, yes! That *is* better. I didn't realise till you said it, but . . .'

She had an uncanny way of knowing when to speak and when to keep quiet. Never before, in his past life or in his current existence, had he felt so comfortable in a shared silence. Dammit!

It was in his power to make her feel better now, and he owed her that much. He didn't want to touch her. God knew, he didn't want to do that, for to touch April would be actually, really to know her—and to know her would be never to forget her.

But that was his problem. He'd manage somehow. When the time came for her to leave, he would manage somehow to erase all memory of her.

. . . Ah, how much he would have given, once, to know a girl such as she. But it was too late for him now, far too late.

April thought it was Finn knocking on her door. She was irritated because she didn't want him to see her flushed, blotchy face. But she wasn't going to send him away unanswered, not when he had actually been kind to her this morning.

'If you've brought tea,' she called out, 'would you leave it outside my door, please, Finn. I'm not dressed.'

The door opened, and the brown velvet voice brought her bolt upright. 'It's brandy.'

'Emile! I—oh——'

'Don't panic. I can't see, remember?'

He was standing by the door, a glass of brandy in either hand, smiling at her.

She didn't know what to say at first. It was such a shock, him coming to her like this. 'I—I'm not undressed, actually.'

'Ah, you were just saying that because you didn't want your privacy invaded. I'm sorry, April. I know the feeling.'

Indeed he did. 'I'll make an exception in your case, because you won't know how dreadful I look.'

His laughter was low, rumbling. 'Will you take these drinks from me and tell me where the chair is?'

April got to her feet and took the glasses. 'The chair's by the dressing table, immediately to your left. About three feet away.'

She waited until he was seated before giving back one of the glasses, prolonging the small talk because she didn't want to know why he'd come to her room. It had to be something serious for him actually to seek her out. 'How come you're having brandy? I'm the one who's unwell!'

She backed away from him, watching him follow her voice as she sat down on the bed. He was orientating himself with the room, a room he couldn't be all that familiar with. 'Sorry, that was my little joke. I'm actually feeling much better.'

'There are flowers in the room.'

'Yes, they're straight ahead of you. On the windowsill. But the curtains are closed. I'm surprised you can smell them.' She got up again, babbling nervously. 'I'll open the curtains. I picked the flowers in the woods this morning. I got up early today. I——'

'April, please relax.' Emile held up a silencing hand

and the false smile dropped from April's face. 'Don't try to be bright and perky when you're feeling unwell. You're fooling no one.'

She sat down again, sipping at her drink in the hope that it would give her the ability to behave normally, casually. It wasn't easy, now she'd finally admitted to herself that she loved him. She'd already made a mess of his day, and now he was here to say something about her work. 'I—I'm sorry about the dictation, Emile. But we can make up for it tomorrow, surely?'

Her remark saddened him. Did she really think he was here to talk about something so unimportant? Or was this just April being April, as thoughtful as ever?

'I'm not here to talk about work.'

'Then—then why are you here?'

'Are you going to make this difficult for me? It isn't easy to apologise, you know. Not for a man like me.'

She frowned, pleased but slightly confused. 'What is a man like you, Emile?'

'A man who has forgotten his manners, simply because he hasn't needed them for a long time. A man who's never before apologised for his behaviour. Behaviour which must seem unnecessarily cold or extremely eccentric to a perceptive girl like you.' He swirled his brandy around in the glass then took a deep swallow.

This wasn't easy for him, she knew that. He was granting her a glimpse of another of his layers. One which lay deeper under the surface. But what did it mean? What was it worth? Very little, if anything at all.

April closed her eyes, squeezing them tightly against the fresh bout of tears which were threatening. Dear

God, she prayed, don't let me show any emotion, for he will sense it, he will hear it, it will reach out to him across the distance which separates us. And I don't want that to happen.

She cleared her throat. 'There's a contradiction there somewhere. If I'm as perceptive as you seem to think then surely I understand your behaviour?' Fool that she was, she thought she was fit to challenge him then. She thought she could go on to tell him she knew all his secrets, that deep down inside he cared for nothing and no one. But she couldn't; it wouldn't hurt him, but it would give her more pain than she could tolerate just now. Instead she held her silence. There was safety in silence.

He shrugged. 'I daresay you understand to some extent. You probably have your own theories. But understanding my shabby treatment of you, my anti-social silences, doesn't mean you like it. I heard the hurt in your voice just now. I've heard it many times before. And I apologise. I've done nothing to make you relaxed and at ease in your temporary home. Apart from that I've piled a lot of extra work on you this past week, and I'm sure all this has contributed to your feeling so tense today. April, will you show me you accept my apology by having lunch with me today?'

April's mouth fell open. She received the apology, and the invitation, with very mixed feelings. Suddenly she wanted to keep up the barriers between them. She did not want the opportunity of getting closer to that core. Not when it was frozen solid. Not when her journey would be painful and pointless.

'I'd be delighted to have lunch with you.' Her eyes closed involuntarily this time. She was immediately rationalising, of course. She was telling herself she had accepted the offer because his pride was at stake. He'd apologised, hadn't he? So how could she possibly have refused him?

'What are you wearing, April? A dress, a skirt—or what?'

She opened her eyes. She hadn't heard a word. 'I'm sorry—what did you say?'

'I'm about to massage your headache away—it's phase two of making April feel better. Come.' He got to his feet, patted the seat of the chair. 'Take off your dress or whatever. Sit here.'

She gaped at him in disbelief. Oh, no! That was too much to ask. To feel his hands on her would be more than she could possibly cope with.

'Don't be silly! I've told you I'm feeling better! Much!' Her heart was pounding like a mad thing, panic making her voice come out in a squeak.

'You lie,' he said simply. 'Modesty with a blind man would be rather foolish, don't you think? Come along, and bear in mind that I studied anatomy many moons ago. The physiology of the female is something I'm very familiar with. Put yourself in my hands and your headache will be gone in five minutes.'

While he waited for her to move she waited for inspiration. What the devil could she say? He'd already cancelled out any logical refusal she might give him!

With hands that were trembling and legs which had suddenly turned to lead she made herself move towards him, pulling off her sweater as she got near him. She sat tentatively on the chair as he moved behind her, feeling certain this would only increase the tension within her.

It didn't. His long, strong fingers got to work on the delicate muscles at the top of her shoulders with a touch which was not gentle. The fingers probed, kneaded, coaxed, and within seconds April felt the benefit. He gave her an occasional instruction as he worked with an expertise which shouldn't have surprised her. 'Let your head fall forward . . . Now let it rest against my hands.' He moved her head from side to side. Then he massaged the upper vertebrae with blissful, circular movements that drained every ounce of tension from her.

April felt marvellous. She flopped against the chair like a rag doll as his hands came to rest lightly on top of her shoulders. 'Better?'

'Oh, yes! Thank you!' Without thought, her hand came up to cover his in a gesture of appreciation. He held her hand in both of his, moving in front of her and pulling her gently to her feet.

Not a word was spoken as she stood looking up at him, a willing captive in the aura of sheer magnetism that emanated from him, that filled any room he happened to be in. When Emile Jacquot was around there was always magic in the air. For April. Even his sadness drew her like a magnet.

His hands reached out to cup her face, the cool fingers a soothing balm against her flushed skin. His fingertips moved lightly over the bone structure, tracing a path from her chin to the gentle curve of her jawbone, over her temples to her forehead. April couldn't have uttered a sound even if she'd wanted to; she welcomed his touch with everything in her. This was Emile saying hello, seeing her for the first time.

She tried not to read anything else into his actions. But the movements of his fingertips suddenly became exquisitely erotic as they moved over her lips, her closed eyelids. Behind the closed eyes there came the unbidden memory of Emile standing naked by the swimming pool. Then, she had felt no stirring of desire; she had looked upon him detachedly as the distant, moving statue that he had been.

It was different now, so very different. There was nothing to separate them, no distance, no words. April would have given him anything now, willingly and unashamedly she would have given all of her. His hands were on her neck, her throat, moving lightly along the soft curve of her shoulders to her arms. On his face there was that familiar look of concentration, his eyes were closed, and her heart was beating so loudly she was afraid it would break the spell.

In those few moments she knew the meaning of pure desire. But there was no desire on his part, she knew that, and when his fingers trailed lightly over the thin material covering her breasts, it was more than she could bear. 'Emile, I—please——'

His eyes flew open instantly, locking on to hers in a silent apology.

'Emile, no! Don't look like that. Don't be sorry!'

A sad smile pulled at the corners of his mouth. 'You're very kind, April.' He moved away from her. 'Very kind and very, very beautiful.'

'Oh!' The cry tore from her because the moment was spoiled, destroyed! 'No! Don't say that. I'm not beautiful, Emile. I'm *not*!'

He opened the door, turning to face her with a lingering smile. 'Ah, my dear April, haven't you learned yet that beauty in a person comes from more than one source?'

April sank down on to the bed. Kind? He'd been the kind one in coming to visit her, in trying to make her feel better.

The time had come when she must give. She realised that now. Since admitting her feelings for him she had behaved very thoughtlessly, had been so concerned with self, with her own feelings, that she hadn't stopped to consider what she might possibly be able to do for Emile.

He liked her, of that she was sure. Why else would he have taken such trouble? All right, maybe he'd done it because he thought that she was discontented, that he might be in danger of losing a good secretary. But at least that was something! It was by no means all she wanted but it was all she had. And with the small amount of power it gave her she would try her level best to show Emile that life was worth living.

Somehow she had to stir him to life again. Somehow she had to show him he could still be happy even if he couldn't paint. It was a very tall order indeed. And it was probably impossible, but she had to try. She *had* to. Besides, wasn't that what love was all about? Giving. She would do anything for those she loved. And she loved Emile more than anything in the world.

At least she had time. She needed it, too, for she would have to tread softly, take it step by step. The first step would be to win his trust. His complete trust. Then she would try her damnedest to get him out of Serena House and into a world which still had plenty to offer him, if he would only open himself to its possibilities.

From now on she would not stop to think of herself. She would think only of him. If there were times when she needed to use a little cunning, or to swallow her pride, she would do it. She would do anything at all in an effort to chip away the ice from that frozen heart. And she would do it in the name of love.

CHAPTER SEVEN

HAVING lunch with the Count provided April with her first real opportunity of getting to know something about him. They talked about one another—nothing too personal or deep, just general details which made conversation flow easily. April thought it strange really, knowing so little about Emile when she knew him so well. It was rather like having lunch with a good friend one hasn't seen for twenty years; the basic understanding was there, they were just catching up on events.

'So how come you choose to live in England?' Emile had just confirmed that he was half English, on his mother's side, but he had been brought up and educated in Paris.

'Well, I inherited this house from my parents. It was left to them by my maternal grandmother, Lady Balfour. My parents retired here when I was twenty. I was in University and had no desire to leave France. Mother had spent twenty-five years in Paris, with my father, and had always promised herself she would end her days in her native England, which she did.

'I'd always loved this house. I came here often to visit my parents, lots of my childhood holidays were spent here, and I know every inch of the place. I've always liked England, and so it seemed ... it seemed logical to come and live here, in a place so familiar and loved, after I lost my sight.'

There were gaps in the story, of course. Surely his home in Paris had been equally familiar and loved? So why move? Probably because by leaving Paris he was leaving behind his past as a painter. And what of his wife? Had she been with him here in the early days? Emile hadn't mentioned her, and it was more than April dared do to broach that particular subject. She was treading carefully as it was.

'What about your relatives? You must have family on both sides of the Channel, how come they don't visit you here?'

Emile shrugged. 'They did in the beginning. But one by one they've got the message that I don't want any intrusion.'

'Now who's beating about the bush? You mean one by one you've frightened them off!'

'All right,' he grinned, 'one by one I've frightened them off.'

'And what about Finn? Where does he fit in?'

'Oh, Finn came into service at Serena House when he was fourteen. He's sixty-four now, would you believe? He worked for my grandmother, then my parents, and I was damned if I could let him go when I inherited. I took him to Paris. We closed Serena House when my parents died. Finn was with me for the three years prior to the accident. After the accident we came back here and—well, you know the rest.'

She knew the rest? There was still no mention of his wife!

Finn came in then. He was carrying a tray on which there was a large bowl of fresh fruit salad, dishes and a jug of cream. He placed everything on the table meticulously, telling his master what he had brought and where everything was. April dished up the salad, noticing Finn's look of approval as she replaced everything in its original position.

Emile refilled their wineglasses. 'I was just telling Miss Baxter you've been with the family since you were fourteen. Isn't that right, Finn?'

The look Finn gave to her then was one of astonishment. 'You were?' It was as if he thought she had achieved something fantastic by culling this sort of information. She winked at him mischievously and Finn didn't know where to put himself.

April smiled. So he was not so inscrutable after all!

'Er—that's right, monsieur. I left school at fourteen and Lady Balfour took me on. 'Course, in those days we had a full staff at the house. Your grandparents were always entertaining and there was hardly a time when we didn't have people staying. Yourself included, sir.' Having said his piece, Finn left as unobtrusively as he had entered.

'And what did your father do, Emile? I mean in Paris, before he retired?'

The Count grimaced slightly. 'He was a politician. Oh, the stories I could tell you! And during the war he was a leading figure in the French Resistance.'

'Really?' April was immediately intrigued. 'No doubt you heard stories about that, too. Is that where you get some of your ideas for your books? From your father's adventures during the war?'

'Some of them, yes. From there and from Finn's army stories. He saw a lot of action during the war, you know. And believe it or not, he tells a good tale, old Finn.'

April couldn't help laughing. 'No, I don't believe it!' She confessed to him then about the private nickname she'd given Finn.

Emile laughed heartily. 'Let's just say that Finn is a very cautious man. He doesn't trust easily.'

'Neither do you.' The words just popped out.

There was a momentary silence. It was not an awkward silence. Emile let it hang in the air between them and April recognised it as a warning. She could go so far and no farther. She accepted it, too . . . for the time being.

When next he spoke, Emile changed the subject completely. He started asking April about herself, about her childhood and her parents.

After lunch April went to her room to have the sleep she was very much in need of. It was almost five when she woke up and she congratulated herself on having made the first small adjustment to a very difficult situation. The pain was still there, and in her heart it would remain, but at least she was learning to live with it. She had made just a tiny bit of progress too, in the promise she'd made herself about Emile.

She showered and slipped into the slacks and sweater she had worn in the early hours of the morning. Had she really gathered flowers in the woods only today? It seemed like a week ago!

When she got halfway down the stairs, April stopped in her tracks. From the drawing room there came the sound of a piano playing Chopin. April was familiar with it. It was a piece which was popularly known as 'So Deep is the Night' when set to a lyric. But never before, in the classical or popular version, had she heard such poignancy in the music.

It wasn't that which halted her, though. It was Finn. He was standing in the hall, outside the closed door of the drawing room, and when April appeared he turned around slowly and smiled at her, actually smiled at her!

She was at once baffled and delighted. A smile from Finn was high praise indeed, but she had no idea why he had granted her this honour. As she moved forward he held a finger to his lips, beckoning her into the kitchen.

She followed him wordlessly, at a complete loss to understand his odd behaviour. When they were safely inside the kitchen she whispered to him, 'What is it? I'm sure I've heard the Count playing records before. Why are you looking so pleased with yourself?'

'That isn't a record, miss.' He turned away, offering to make her some tea, but April caught hold of his arm.

'It's Monsieur Jacquot? But what does this mean, Finn? Tell me, please!'

He shrugged, his massive shoulders hunched in an attitude of uncertainty. 'I'm not sure. All I can tell you is that he hasn't touched a piano in five years.'

April stared at him. 'Why, this is wonderful! Please, I want you to tell me something. Please don't be evasive. Please trust me.' She was plunging right in while the going was good. 'What happened with his wife—the divorce?'

But Finn was having none of that. The shutters dropped over his face and he turned abruptly away from her. 'I'll make the tea. I've got some cream cakes in the fridge, would you like one, miss?'

April sank on to a kitchen chair. It had been worth a try, but she'd been expecting too much of him. She brightened, thinking she could perhaps try a different tack. 'No, thanks. I'm already overweight.'

She thought he muttered something about stuff and nonsense. 'Will you join me in a cup of tea, Finn? You're always on the go. Can you spare ten minutes?'

'I don't mind if I do, miss.'

When they were settled at the kitchen table she tried again. The music had changed, but as long as it continued, she was safe. 'What happened at the time of the accident? I mean, do you know the details? They didn't say much in the newspapers.'

Finn let out a long, slow breath. She feared he had lost patience with her, and was astonished at his answer. 'Of course I know the details. I was in the plane with him.'

'Oh! I—I'm sorry, I had no idea.'

'That's all right. I've dreamt about it often enough. It doesn't bother me to talk of it. It was a small private aircraft. We were flying from Paris to London for the preview of Jacquot's first exhibition here. There were just the two of us and the pilot. There'd been a fuel leakage. 'Course, the pilot had no idea of this; something was wrong with the instrument panel and it didn't register. The engine started coughing and spluttering and the poor sod—excuse me—the pilot did all he could to get us down safely. We made a crash landing in a field in Devon.

'Monsieur Jacquot was almost unhurt. I was trapped. I knew my leg was broken. It was twisted, trapped underneath my seat and there was no feeling in it. The Count freed me, dragged me well away from the wreckage before the damn thing went up in flames. After getting me in the clear he went back for the pilot. I yelled at him. Over and over I yelled for him to come back, but he didn't hear me, or he ignored me. But he never made it anyway. When he got within a few yards of the wreckage there was an almighty explosion which nearly cost him his life, let alone his sight.'

There was a silence as they both saw it all happening, Finn for the millionth time, no doubt. 'You—you'd seen it coming, of course, the explosion?'

'Yes, miss. But it wasn't only that. You see . . . you see, the pilot was already dead. Monsieur Jacquot didn't know that. But I'd seen his face. I looked at that death mask when the Count was busy freeing me.'

The soft music was still drifting into the kitchen. Finn didn't move. April covered her face with her hands and kept them there as the full implication of Finn's words sank in.

It was a long time before she could find her voice. 'Is there no hope at all? His sight . . . I mean, did they tell him—what about in the future, an operation perhaps? Didn't they give him any hope?'

Finn shrugged. 'He's adjusted now. He's lived with it for five years.'

'That doesn't answer my question.'

The elderly servant looked at her as if he were almost afraid to tell her. 'Well, a couple of years after the accident, he got a letter. I read it to him. It was from a Swiss professor, an old friend of the family. He's a pioneer in new techniques, an eye specialist. He asked Monsieur Jacquot to go to his clinic in Switzerland for an examination. He promised nothing, of course, just asked to examine the Count.'

April leaned forward eagerly. 'Well? What happened?'

The watery blue eyes looked at her hopelessly. 'Monsieur Jacquot put the letter on the fire.'

'*What*? He didn't go? He didn't even see whether——?'

'A couple of weeks later he sent his cousin to Switzerland—to deliver a painting. It was a strange thing to do, I thought. He sent no reply, just one of his paintings. It was one of his most famous, too, the one set in the orchard, you know.'

'I know it. I have a copy of it in my flat.' April shook her head incredulously. 'Was that the end of the matter?'

'Not quite. There was another letter from the Professor. About a week later, I think. It—it was a stream of abuse which just made the Count laugh. You can guess what he did with it. The Professor didn't give up. He phoned here about a month later. 'Course, I've no idea what was said.'

'Has there been any contact since?'

'Not a word.'

April's hands tightened into fists. 'I don't under-stand it, Finn. I just don't understand it.'

'Well, I do,' he shrugged. 'The Professor offered nothing other than an examination. But the Count's made his adjustment now. He won't dare to allow himself even to hope he might be helped. Besides, the hospital in London told him categorically that there was no hope, not ever. So I can understand it. I—I did try talking to him at the time, miss, but he bit my head off. He said it's something he *knows*, deep down inside, that he'll be blind for the rest of his life.'

April looked at him helplessly, even fondly. 'You don't exactly have it easy here. You're on duty seven nights a week. But you don't stay because the Count saved your life, do you?'

'Oh, no, miss! And if the Count thought that about me, he'd never allow me to serve him. I stay because I've always been devoted to the family, and he knows that.'

Emile withdrew into his own private world again. But
April expected it, and she doubled up on her efforts to
communicate, to reach him. She stayed at Serena
House over the weekend and did manage to join Emile
for a brief walk in the grounds but he kept his distance
even as they strolled side by side.

As the days unfolded it seemed that she was fighting
a losing battle; it was almost as if the Count were
resisting her every inch of the way. Finn's revelation
had sickened her and her love for Emile grew deeper
and stronger with every passing day, and not once did
she falter in the impossible task she had set herself.

The following weekend she went home and picked
up her post, a few bills, her agency cheque and a
programme of the forthcoming operas at the Coliseum.
She dusted the flat, did a little washing and ironing.
Nearly all her clothes were at Serena House now,
together with most of her records and cassettes.

She went on to Alan's and met the Scottish
housekeeper, who was now hired and had made herself
quite at home in what used to be the guest room. April
was obliged to sleep in her niece's room, but she
didn't mind that; she was only too glad to find the
housekeeper so pleasant and obviously getting on well
with Alan and the children.

Mrs MacGregor, or Moira, as she preferred to be
called, was a woman in her early forties and had a son
of her own. She had been widowed when the boy was
three and had spent all her subsequent years as a
housekeeper. Her son was now nineteen and attending
London University, where he was training to become
a doctor. Moira, quite justifiably, was very proud of
him. Her life could not have been an easy one.

Alan seemed much more relaxed now the strain had

been taken from him. It pleased April to see this, to see him eating well and getting on very compatibly with his now housekeeper. In six weeks his life had changed so much for the better . . . Six weeks? Was it only six weeks since that fateful day when April had walked into the library of Serena House to meet the Count Emile Jacquot de Nîmes? It was amazing, almost frightening to think how much could happen in so short a time.

The month of April drew to a close, with nature taking her course predictably and beautifully. The gardens of Serena House were already abundant with flowers and the promise of more to come. April looked forward to seeing the rose garden in full bloom. She promised herself she would stroll through it with Emile and paint for him in words everything she could see. How she looked forward to that!

April's patience was rewarded when the Count finally asked her to dine with him. They had been working for barely half an hour and he seemed to be in a rather testy sort of mood, so the last thing she expected was an invitation to dinner.

She was reading aloud the previous day's dictation. As ever, she was almost acting it out, putting what she thought was the right emotion into the words. '. . . Sharkey kept absolutely still. They were hunting for him. He couldn't hear them, he couldn't see them, but he knew they were there. His only chance was in keeping silent, motionless. His thoughts turned to Mary, and he vowed that if the ever got safely back to England he would marry that girl—give up this stinking life. He could see her now as clearly as if she were lying beside him; he could smell the delicate perfume of her hair, feel the smooth silk of her skin beneath his——'

'Cut that!' The Count's command brought her head up sharply.

'I'm sorry?'

'I said cut it. Scrub it. The whole page—it's rubbish!'

'Oh!' April was taken aback. 'It seems a shame to do that. I thought it was rather nice, Sharkey reminiscing. It makes him more human——'

'It's out of character,' Emile snapped. 'He's not supposed to be human. Cut it!' And with that, he spun his chair round to face the window.

April waited. And waited. 'I—I've done it, Emile. I'm ready if you are.'

He turned with an apologetic look on his face. 'April . . . April, will you dine with me tonight?'

'Why—yes, I'd be delighted to.'

He seemed doubtful. 'Would you, April? I mean, don't you——'

Finn came in then, and April was as surprised at the interruption as the Count was annoyed.

'What is it, Finn?'

'I'm sorry, Monsieur Jacquot, but your publisher's on the phone. He says it's urgent.' He shot April an enquiring glance and she shrugged, unable to account for Emile's unprecedented display of emotion.

'What the hell does he want at this hour? It's barely eight o'clock. He should know I'm working now!'

'He apologised for that. Said something about going out of town today.'

'All right, all right. I'll take it in April's office. Ask him to hold on a minute.'

When Finn had gone, Emile turned to her. 'April, take the day off. I can't write today—I'm not in the mood. Go for a drive or something—but I will see you in the drawing room at seven?'

'Of course.' She was at a loss to understand him but wasn't going to show it. She got up and headed for the door.

'And April . . . wear something nice.'

Wear something nice? Now she was even more confused!

CHAPTER EIGHT

WHEN she met him in the drawing room some of April's confusion vanished. Emile was standing by the fireplace, wearing full evening dress and looking superb. In a maroon velvet jacket and a lacy white shirt he looked every inch the aristocrat. With the touches of grey in his hair he looked distinguished, too, and very dignified.

On seeing him April felt a constriction in her throat. How she loved him, handsome, talented . . . and unattainable.

Hearing her, he turned instantly, coming across the room to take her hands in his. 'April, I'm honoured by your company.'

She laughed shyly. 'I think I'm the one who's honoured! Do you always dress so splendidly for dinner?'

'Er—no! I always change, of course, but I don't normally go to such trouble.'

'Then why tonight?' He still had hold of her hands.

'Tonight is special. Today is the first of May.'

'So . . .?'

'So it is your birthday, *n'est-ce pas?*'

She was both pleased and disappointed. Pleased that he had remembered such a detail but disappointed because this invitation was obviously made from a sense of duty—and she'd thought he simply wanted her company.

'I hope you like champagne, April? I have on ice the very best France has to offer.'

'I love it!'

There was the popping of a champagne cork and then a toast, a little speech made in French which went right over her head.

'Oh, dear!' April giggled. 'I don't know what you're saying, but I'm sure it's nice!'

Emile looked at her in mock disdain. 'I'm toasting your health, the completion of twenty-four years, and wishing you many happy years ahead.'

He motioned her towards the settee nearest the fire and sat beside her. 'You must have learned the language in school. Tell me, how good is your French?'

She picked her word deliberately, remembering only too well his opening sentence to her at the interview. 'Mediocre.'

He saw it at once and laughed loudly. 'Oh, April! Never be mediocre. If you do something—anything— you must do it well. You must excel!'

'It's a nice idea, but my dear Emile, we are not all as gifted as you.'

'There's only one way to learn French,' he said, still laughing. 'Go to France! Tell me, have you ever seen Paris?'

'No. I've never been to France.'

He put his hands on his heart as if she had wounded him. 'That's terrible! Terrible! And we must do something . . . you must do something about that.'

It seemed the champagne went right to April's head. She was relaxed, happy, and within minutes Emile had her talking about herself again.

'You were telling me the other day that your parents had ideas of putting you on the stage when you were little. What happened?'

'Nothing happened.' She smiled. 'I grew up, that's all! And with that process it became obvious I had neither the looks nor the talent to set the world alight. As I told you, I'm not the beauty you seem to think I am.' It was important to April to reiterate this. She didn't want him having any illusions about her.

His voice was quiet then, soft and serious. 'And I've told you, beauty comes from within.'

The remark pleased her, naturally, because she knew he was sincere. Apart from that, he was making a charming effort to make her birthday happy.

'So what of your piano lessons?'

'They fizzled out eventually, although they lasted longer than my ballet class and tap-dancing lessons.'

'You had singing lessons, too.'

She looked at him in surprise. 'Yes, but how did you know? I had all the nice little extras a well brought up young woman has. But it didn't come to anything.'

'I've heard you,' he said then.

'Sorry?'

'I've heard you singing in the bath. And very nice it is, too.'

'Oh, *no*!' She didn't know where to put herself, was acutely embarrassed. 'You can't have! The walls in this house are too thick——'

'Calm yourself.' He roared with laughter, reached for the cigarette box and offered her one. '*Ma chère Avril*, I can hear the grass grow! You should know that by now. Come.'

'Come where?'

'To the piano, of course. You will sing for your supper.'

'I will not!'

'Then you will sing for me.'

'I certainly will not!' But she got up, pleased to dispose of the ghastly cigarette he'd given her. It gave off a nice aroma, but it tasted horrible. 'However, I'll join you in a duet.'

They squeezed together on the piano stool and Emile looked at her expectantly. 'Right. What'll it be?'

She said the first thing that popped into her head. 'Er—"Moonlight becomes you". Do you know it?'

'I know it,' he grinned. 'But that's an after-dinner song. It will go down better with liqueurs. Right now we want something bubbly.' He thought for a moment. 'Okay, since you're sitting on the left, give me an eight-bar boogie on the bass notes.'

She gasped as if horrified. 'We can't play boogie-woogie on a Steinway grand!'

'Why ever not? The instrument is here for our pleasure. Play, woman, play!'

April did as she was told. Five minutes later she was giving full voice to 'The Boogie-Woogie Washerwoman' ... until she had a sudden mental picture of Finn in the kitchen, and the look on his face. At which point she collapsed in hysterics and when she was able to tell Emile what she was thinking he ended up roaring with laughter, too.

Finn had excelled himself. Dinner was superb, and by the time they were half way through it April was bordering on intoxication. And it wasn't only from the champagne and the wines.

When Emile handed her a small, beautifully wrapped box she sobered somewhat. 'For me? Oh— I—Emile, you shouldn't have!'

'But of course I should. It's just a small gesture of appreciation. Go on, open it!'

The small gesture of appreciation was a solid silver

necklace in the shape of a butterfly on a fine chain. It was absolutely exquisite and April was very touched. 'It's beautiful! I—thank you, Emile.'

'What are you wearing tonight? A dress?'

'Yes. It's midnight blue with a scoop neck. The necklace will set it off beautifully.' She fastened the necklace, put it in place and reached for Emile's hand. 'See?'

He nodded slowly, his gentle fingers moving lightly over the chain at her neck and the butterfly which felt cool and heavy against the base of her throat.

Finn, also, had a contribution to make. To her birthday and to her happiness. When he brought in the dessert he handed her a large box of handmade chocolates. 'Many happy returns, miss! And don't you go telling me you daren't eat those things!'

Foolish tears sprang to her eyes as she thanked him warmly. How sweet of them, both of them! Finn must have chosen the necklace on the Count's instructions. And how thoughtful of him to give her a gift from himself. She looked from one man to the other and wished fervently that she belonged, really belonged, at Serena House, that this birthday dinner was not being given to her solely as a matter of duty.

They didn't play the piano after dinner. The mood had changed and they went back to the drawing room, quite content to sit by the fire and talk over coffee.

'Was something wrong this morning? I mean, that phone call from your publisher. Was he asking when the book will be ready?'

'No, no. Old Max was in quite a lather, actually. He's been contacted by an American film company. They want to make a film of my last book.'

'Really? Gosh, that's exciting, isn't it!'

'Is it?' He didn't seem bothered one way or the other.

She looked at him in surprise. 'Well, of course it is! It'll be nice for your fans.'

He didn't seem to know what she was talking about. 'Fans?'

'Your readers, silly! I'm sure they'd all go and see the film version of one of your stories.'

Emile lit a cigarette, considering this. 'Yes, I suppose that's one way of looking at it.'

'I think so. Besides, you sort of owe it to them. Not to refuse, I mean.'

'I didn't refuse. It's entirely up to Max. It'll make him a lot of money.'

April smiled to herself. Emile was in the position of not having to consider the money it would make for himself.

'I don't mind,' he assured her. 'I'm told it would only necessitate giving a small amount of my time. A few consultations with the author . . . they could come here . . .' He finished the thought to himself and April looked at him askance. He was thinking about his blasted routine being upset! His self-imposed imprisonment being invaded!

So it was just as she thought! Emile didn't give a damn for Jason Jordan, either. His writing was just a catharsis, a means of giving vent to that which was his innermost layer—his anger. She was recalling Finn's revelation, the way Emile had lost his sight unnecessarily—in an effort to save a dead man. Dear Lord, no wonder he needed an outlet!

She put a smile into her voice. 'You know, I once asked you how long you'd been writing and you gave me a very—er—ungentlemanly reply! And it was an innocent question. I was only wondering, then, how long you'd been writing as Jason Jordan.'

His eyes were brown now, sparkling and full of amusement. 'I remember. And the answer to your current question is yes, I used to write before I was blind, purely for my own entertainment. I used to write poetry. Are you satisfied now?'

April didn't comment. With every passing day she was learning more and more about Emile. But she was not about to let him know how much she had learned. Not yet. One day she would use all her knowledge to shake this man to his very foundations. She would bring him to life even if she had to hurt him terribly in the process. But she must bide her time. At the moment she didn't have enough power, enough influence to make even the smallest impression.

She reached for his hand. It was a deliberate, calculated action—though it came very easily to her, of course. 'My dear Emile, I must bid you goodnight now. Thank you for a wonderful evening.'

He gave her that special smile which always made her feel as if the sun had just appeared, and as they stood he kept hold of her hand. 'Goodnight, April. Thank you. I enjoyed it, too.'

'Did you? You know, you're quite a puzzle. For someone who said he's forgotten his manners I've found you to be the perfect host. But you made me wait a long time for the privilege of spending an evening with you. And you only invited me this evening because it's my birthday.'

'No, that's not true. Your birthday was a good excuse, that's all. An excuse to impinge on your privacy.'

'I'm not the one who has a need for privacy, Emile. If you were willing, I'd dine with you every night.'

'Ah, *ma chère Avril*.' He lifted her hand to his lips. 'You're so kind.'

'Kindness has nothing to do with it. You've really been quite selfish, you know. You apologised for your anti-social behaviour and then you withdrew from me completely! I have needs, too. I thought you'd realised that. If you really want me to be happy here you must give me more of your company.'

His dark eyebrows drew together in a frown. 'Is that what you want? Really?'

She had little pride as far as he was concerned, and even if she hadn't been doing this deliberately she doubted whether she'd have given him a different answer. 'Yes. It's what I want. It's what I need.'

He smiled, seeming pleased but still slightly doubtful. 'Until tomorrow evening, then.'

'Until tomorrow evening, Emile.'

With that, he let go of her hand and April left him in the drawing room. She took the stairs to her bedroom two at a time, knowing she had broken down a barrier. She was flushed, excited, and under her breath she was chanting, 'Colour me pink. Colour me pink. Colour me pink, pink, pink!'

CHAPTER NINE

From that day onwards they were never apart. They worked together as secretary and boss and lunched and dined together as friends. They played the piano often, although April preferred to sit and listen rather than to participate. Emile was good, really good. But then he would be, April reflected. Emile was a very talented man. Anything he put his mind to he would master—he would excel in!

They swam together, naked. April was shy at first until Emile lectured her on the beauty of the female form, insisting she should never be ashamed of her nakedness.

'I'm not!' She'd made a half-hearted protest. 'And I know you can't see, but I know what I look like and I'm—well, let's say there's just a little more of me than I'd like!'

'What nonsense!' he'd scoffed. 'I have seen you, remember? And I think you're perfect.'

'Rubensesque?' she giggled.

'Oh, April, don't exaggerate so!'

They talked at length about art, mainly about French painters whom they both favoured. *With the exception of one.* They talked music, politics and history and Emile was a veritable mine of information when it came to the subject of wines. He took her into his wine cellars, with Finn trailing behind because he knew where everything was stacked. In the cellars was a fortune in vintage wines and champagnes and day by

day, over meals, April's knowledge grew and her
tastebuds became more discerning. 'Don't forget,'
Emile said, 'that in the end wines are for drinking,
enjoying. One mustn't take the hoarding bit too
far.'

They walked round the extensive grounds, come
showers or sun, and when May slipped into June the
roses came into their own. But April didn't paint the
rose garden for him in words, as she'd planned to.
Emile did that for her. She shouldn't have been
surprised, really. It was no exaggeration that Emile
knew every inch of the gounds as well as he knew
Serena House. The gardeners had their work cut out
for them now and did a splendid job of keeping the
lawns like fresh green carpets. When June moved into
July everything in the garden was perfect, abundant.
April cut roses and put them in every downstairs
room, which necessitated Finn going out to buy bowls
and more vases. But he was only too pleased to do it; it
was clear by now that he approved very much of April.
Emile approved very much of having flowers in the
house. He would always ask exactly where they were
placed and what kind of container they were in.

April didn't visit her brother as often as she used to.
Really, Alan was getting along beautifully and had no
need of her. Her visits to Surrey became almost duty
calls in order to see the children. Emile always asked
about them, took an interest in what the children had
been doing. More than once April had invited him to
join her when she took the children out, but he never
did.

The book wasn't going as well as it should. Some
days Emile would skip work completely and they
would take a late breakfast on the lawn by the

swimming pool, bathing in the morning sun with April reading the paper to her companion. Of course April was pleased that the book was progressing so slowly. As far as she was concerned Emile could take five years to complete it.

She was deliriously happy, except for the knowledge that this beautiful time would have to end one day. That was the only cloud in her otherwise blue sky. But as the days unfolded she became hopeful. Emile was enjoying himself, she felt sure of that. And if his writing continued at such a slow pace maybe he would take her on permanently? She could hope for nothing more than that because it was painfully obvious that Emile was not interested in her physically, romantically. In fact it had got to the stage when they hardly touched one another now. Any attempt she made to take Emile's hand, or even his arm, was rejected in the politest way. Nothing was said; it was just that he avoided her touch, and the shutters would close over his face. To April this was hurtful, especially since he used once to reach for her hand so spontaneously. But she accepted it and didn't try to alter things in any way; she did not want to risk any kind of withdrawal at this stage.

She loved him to the point of distraction, to the point where she could not allow herself to think of the day she would have to leave. But any hopes she had nurtured of Emile taking her on permanently were shattered when his publisher, Max, called at the house. Max had telephoned first, to say he wanted to talk to Emile about the American film and about his future work. The two men spent the entire afternoon in the library—and April was not invited to sit in, not even to take notes. It was obvious, therefore, that any future plans Emile was making did not include his current secretary.

Having prior knowledge of this, which she had had from the very beginning, did not lessen her longing to spend the rest of her life with the man she loved. It seemed that she had got far more from the relationship than Emile. April hadn't intended this to happen, it just did. Emile was a wonderful conversationalist and very knowledgeable. Contrary to what she had hoped to achieve it was he, in fact, who opened up new worlds for her.

As for Emile, well, it was difficult to tell how much progress she'd made as far as her private project was concerned. Certainly Emile appeared to be happier these days, but despite the fact that they spent so much time together, he still hadn't allowed her to know what was really in his mind, how he really felt about life. Their conversations never went deeper than general topics. It was as if there were a part of himself which he refused to share with anyone. He was still very much a mystery.

It was on the second Saturday in July that April went shopping for the outfit she would wear to Shirley's wedding. She met Shirley at Marble Arch in the early afternoon and together they trudged from store to store in an effort to find something really special for the big day.

'We should have done this earlier,' Shirley protested as she pulled a face at the green dress and jacket April was trying on, 'instead of leaving it till a week before the wedding!'

April didn't comment. She would have bought her outfit weeks ago, but Shirley had wanted to help her choose—and Shirley had been in Leeds for the past few weekends. 'Never mind.' She made an effort to placate her friend, taking into account the inevitable pre-wedding nerves. 'We're only halfway down Oxford Street—we've got a hundred more stores to look at before we're defeated!'

It was turned five o'clock before they found just the right thing, and just the right hat to go with it. When at last the garments were paid for and wrapped, the two girls looked at one another with a mixture of satisfaction and weariness. 'Right,' Shirley laughed, 'shall we feed ourselves now?'

'You bet. I'm gasping for a drink and half faint with hunger!' April tucked her parcels under her arm and let Shirley lead the way.

Within twenty minutes they were seated at a corner table in a small Italian restaurant and had ordered much-needed drinks.

'Here's to the wedding!' April giggled, raising her glass in a toast.

'Honestly, I wonder if it's worth it!' Shirley tossed back her long dark hair, her eyes riveted to the menu. 'I mean, I would have been quite content to have a small ceremony in a register office, especially in view of the upheaval of moving north to boot. But it was Paul's parents—would you believe it—who insisted on a big church affair. They wanted to "have the best" for their only son. I ask you!'

April laughed, not at all convinced by the other girl's protests. 'You wanted it, too. Come on, admit it, you'll love every minute of it!' Then, as her laughter faded, she added, 'I'm very happy for you Shirley. I wish you all the luck in the world.'

Something in April's voice brought Shirley's head

up quickly. She put the menu to one side, frowning
slightly. She felt guilty. She'd let the whole afternoon
slip by without asking April how she was getting on.
And now it wasn't difficult to see that something was
wrong. 'April, what were you thinking . . . It's Emile,
isn't it? What—how are you getting on with him?'

'Very well.' April's answer came quickly enough.
She told her friend of the lovely way in which her
relationship with Emile had grown, how he had
invited her to dine with him on her birthday, and how
they had hardly been out of one another's company
ever since. But as she talked, even she could hear the
false gaiety in her voice. And she knew she wasn't
fooling Shirley for one minute. Her voice trailed off in
mid-sentence and she fished in her handbag for a
cigarette, choked by the threat of sudden tears.

'I—I know what you're about to say.' When she
found her voice again she held up a hand in protest. 'I
should have left Serena House weeks ago. I should
never have . . . I'm out of his league, I know that.
Basically, we're worlds apart, that's the trouble, and
I . . .'

The look on Shirley's face made her stop. Shirley
lowered her eyes, stiffening slightly, and the gesture
forced April to acknowledge how stupid and meaning-
less it was to make excuses. Shirley was an intelligent
woman, she'd known April well for some time—so it
wasn't difficult for her to guess the truth.

'B-But that wouldn't make any difference,' April
forced herself to face the situation, 'if he were
interested in me. I know that. I—it's just that——'

'Oh, April!' Shirley leaned over to touch her hand.
'I hate to see you hurting like this. Is there no feeling
on Emile's side? I mean, has he tried to——'

The question hung in the air and April shook her head. 'Physically, he avoids me like the plague. We're friends, and that's all there is to it as far as he's concerned.'

It was good to have someone to talk to. April poured out her heart to sympathetic ears without embarrassment, without holding anything back—and without hope. Shirley was a good friend, too concerned to lie, too honest to offer hope when they both knew there was none.

'I should have seen this coming.' It was Shirley who said it, not April. 'The last time I saw you, when you first told me about him, I should have seen this coming. I realised you liked Emile but—Oh, April I've got to say it, it's hopeless! Cut your losses and get out of there now!'

'But—but don't you think that in time he might . . .' April couldn't finish the question. Not when she knew the answer already. 'Shirley, I've told you my theories about him, about the way he's cut himself off from life, the way he misses painting. I've been trying to show him there are other things to live for—pleasure just in day-to-day living. And I know I've made progress, a lot of progress. So don't you think——'

Despite herself, the question surfaced again.

'No.' Shirley's voice was gentle but firm. 'I don't think he'll fall in love with you given time. That's what you're hoping for. If I were in the same situation, I'd hope for it, too. But can't you see now that my first idea was right? He's still in love with Françoise. From all you've told me—can't you see that now? Emile didn't just cut himself off from life, he cut himself off *emotionally*. There's the real barrier.' She paused as a waiter came to refill their coffee cups, waiting until he was well out of earshot before continuing. 'April, if anyone were able to get through to that man, it's you. I'm sure he likes you very much. Well, that much is obvious, but——'

Shirley didn't finish the sentence. She didn't need to. April finished it to herself. . . . But in all this time, he had given no indication of—there had not been so much as a goodnight kiss.

'I think you've been fooling yourself about him mourning for his painting,' Shirley went on. 'He lost his wife to another man and *that's* what he's never got over.' She shrugged, looking at April sadly, helplessly. 'I'm sorry, but I think you'd be wiser to leave Serena House as quickly as possible.'

'It's all right,' April said quietly. She was not convinced of the accuracy of Shirley's ideas, but the advice was good. There was no denying that. Whether it was her own ideas which were correct, or Shirley's, hardly mattered. The fact remained that Emile would never love her no matter how long she stayed with him.

She walked with Shirley as far as the Underground, feeling a sense of gratitude towards her for being so honest—ruthlessly honest.

'I'll miss you when you move north,' she said, as they were parting to take their separate trains.

'Hey, Leeds isn't a million miles away! You'll come and spend the weekend from time to time, won't you?'

'Of course I will. Cheerio, see you next week. See you in church!'

Shirley didn't laugh. At that moment she looked positively unhappy. 'I'm sorry it's turned out like this for you, April. It all seems so unfair when I'm——' She checked herself, realising how tactless her words

might sound. 'Oh, April, you always were hard to
please as far as men are concerned! And now you've
fallen for one who's so——'

'Uninterested,' April finished for her. 'Yes, and
unattainable. You're right, you're right.'

'Are you going to leave, get another job soon?' A sad
smile touched Shirley's lips even before April
answered her. 'No, you're not. I thought as much!'
She shrugged, at a loss for words.

'I'm hurting myself, I know,' April said softly. 'But
I can't help it. I—I'll have to leave him soon enough
in any case, but I'm not going to leave a minute sooner
than I must.'

CHAPTER TEN

THAT Emile was still in love with his ex-wife was an idea April had given no credence to at first. Now, the conversation in the restaurant with Shirley kept coming back to her. Could it be the case? Could someone carry a torch for five long years?

There was only one way to find out, but April cringed at the thought of it. She could ask Emile about his past, get him to talk about his life as Jacquot. She didn't need to talk about his wife; by getting him to talk about his life as a painter she could find out how he felt, now, about his painting. Then she would know for certain whether her own theories were correct, whether it was in fact the loss of his ability to paint which prevented him from being fully alive.

But the thought of broaching the subject frightened April. Not once had she and Emile talked about Jacquot. It had been understood right from the beginning that he didn't wish to do that. Apart from that, she was afraid that his well-harnessed but deeply rooted anger might be turned upon her if she touched on such a sore subject. There was another consideration—and this was the most frightening of all—if she discovered that Emile had really, truly adjusted to his blindness, then her own theories would go up in smoke. And if she discovered she'd been working on false premises all these months then she would be forced to face the fact that there was no point whatever in remaining at Serena House.

She didn't want to have it made clear to her that there was nothing more she could do for Emile. As long as she had this, a reason for staying, life had meaning.

The days passed inexorably. Shirley's wedding came and went; very successfully, too. Life in Serena House continued as it had throughout the entire, beautiful summer. Emile and April shared glorious days and long, lazy evenings, as friends, as companions. And all the time April clung desperately to the now flimsy excuse that she was staying for Emile's sake. With that in mind she could override the knowledge that she was building up her inevitable heartbreak day by day—because day by day her love for Emile deepened.

It was when July slipped into August that she was forced to make a move, to take her courage into her hands. August! Had Jason Jordan's book been written at his normal pace, she should be leaving Serena House in September. The booking was for six months, give or take a couple of weeks. The book was barely half written, but Emile had made no mention of her employment being continued. And that was another subject April was afraid to broach.

It couldn't continue like this for ever. She knew that. Life is not a vacuum and beautiful summers don't go on for ever. April said these words aloud, one evening as she was dressing for dinner, one evening when she took a long, hard look at herself in the mirror.

She had spent the entire afternoon in bed with a headache. Emile knew what was ailing her, but this time he had made no attempt to massage her tension away. Which was just as well. Now, she would not be able to endure the touch of his hands without reacting, without breaking down and telling him how much she loved him. That was the last thing she wanted to do.

She got to her feet, smoothing down her skirt with nervous hands. The tension inside her was mounting daily, like the power of a volcano—and any time now something would have to give. She just couldn't continue like this.

Tonight. Tonight she would talk about Jacquot. For her own sake. For Emile's sake, too, she must air this subject once and for all. The time had come to try and get him to talk about the past. Then she would know where she stood. As for Emile—well, until he could talk about the past he would never be able to let go of it. What ever it was that haunted him.

She waited until after dinner, until they were sitting in the drawing room. They were sitting quietly, smoking, drinking coffee in an atmosphere which was perfect. April was curled up on the settee, enjoying the sight of Emile in the armchair she had once known he would favour even before she had met him. She was thinking of the first time she had seen the drawing room, how much she had liked it instantly. That thought gave her the perfect means of opening the conversation, of steering the conversation.

'You know, I really love this room.'

Emile smiled. 'Yes, it has good vibes, hasn't it? This house has been a very happy place in the past.'

'Mind you, I like the dining room, too, with its Wedgwood blue and white walls. The décor of the entire house is gorgeous. Who did it?'

'It was done by a firm in London, but I chose the colour schemes. With Finn's assistance, of course! When he got no response to his news, he grinned.

'Aren't you surprised? Or have you realised by now that there's nothing wrong with my imagination or my memory for colour?'

'Long since. What about the furniture? Was it your mother's, or did you bring it with you from . . . from Paris?'

'Some of it's mine. I brought just my favourite pieces, like the satinwood table, that antique mirror over there and the Renoir over the fireplace.'

April was watching him carefully, her stomach contracted into a tight knot. 'And your own paintings.'

He looked up quickly, surprised, as if he were disappointed in her. Then his face tightened and his look changed to one of wariness. 'All right, April,' he said slowly, 'what is it you want to say about Jacquot?'

'About him, nothing in particular. It's you I'm concerned about.'

He seemed pleased she had acknowledged the distinction, but his voice was weary as he spoke. 'So?'

She took a deep breath, afraid he might lose his temper. But that was a risk she'd have to take. 'Well, you've . . . you've kept four Jacquot paintings and it seems—it seems wrong to me. They should be in public galleries. They should be given to the world. Most especially since their number will never be increased.'

She'd started it, and she braced herself. It was a long moment before Emile spoke, and when he did so he used that smooth velvet voice which masked his emotions. Or attempted to. 'Don't I have any rights? Am I not entitled to keep just four of them?'

April thought hard about that. 'Maybe you are. But . . . but you're keeping them for the wrong reasons.' She paused only momentarily, her fingers curled so tightly that her nails were cutting into her palms. 'I think you keep those paintings because you're keeping hold of the past, because you just can't let go of the past.'

It got a reaction. April dreaded it and welcomed it at the same time.

'Why, you little fool! I've spent five years doing precisely that! I *have* let go of the past!' He got up from his chair, started stalking the room in that panther-like way of his. '*Ars longa, vita brevis!* Now will you retract your remark?'

'I—I don't know what you mean.'

'Art is long, life is short. Now do you see?'

'No.'

Suddenly, quite unexpectedly, he calmed down. 'All right, April. Then let me explain. Art lives on. It has an existence of its own and if it's really good it lives on when generations of men have died. I am proud, exultant to have been able to produce such work! I thank God for the gift I had for so many years. But it's gone now, and I accept that totally and completely. I only wish that other people would accept it, too. I shall be blind for the rest of my life. That's something I *know*. The four paintings in this house are here for my pleasure. Believe me, I can see them better than you can. What more could one ask than art giving pleasure? That is its function. When I'm gone, those pieces will be passed into other appreciative hands. It doesn't matter to me whether they go before the public or to an individual. As long as they give pleasure then everything will be as it should. I don't think in terms of owning them, I think in terms of having them on loan. Temporarily they are here to give me pleasure, and that has nothing to do with not letting go of the past.'

It was quite a speech. April looked at him incredulously. He was telling the truth, of that she was certain. He meant every word he'd said. 'So—so you really have adjusted to the fact that you'll never paint again?'

'Yes,' he said firmly, 'I've adjusted.'

April spoke half to herself, still pressing the point. It was as if she couldn't believe it. All these months she'd been wrong in her ideas. Wrong! 'You're saying you're grateful for having been blessed with such a gift, for the ability to produce beauty which will go on existing through generations . . . and your heart no longer aches for its return?'

His smile was wry. 'For the ability to paint, my heart no longer aches.'

He turned away from her then, and April nodded slowly, her eyes stinging with tears. This was it. Her days with Emile were numbered. There was nothing further she could do to help him, except, perhaps . . .

'I see.' Her voice was barely more than a whisper. 'But tell me, why do you remain a prisoner here? Why did you never come out with me?'

He spun around quickly. 'Prisoner? What are you talking about? There's a big difference between being a prisoner and being a hermit! I stay here because I choose to, not because I have to! I like peace and privacy, that's all.'

'Okay,' she challenged, 'prove that to me. Come out with me this week.' She held her breath. She wanted this so much; for him, for her. She wanted just once to get him out of the house, to have a lovely evening with him which she would be able to hold in her memory long after she had left Serena House.

'I don't have to prove anything to anyone, April. You disappoint me. Why the hell should I go out?'

'Because,' she said simply, praying that he cared at least enough to do this one small thing for her, 'I'm asking you to. It would give me a lot of pleasure, Emile.'

She went to bed then, only to spend a sleepless night in a silence that screamed at her, a room which seemed suddenly too hot to breathe in. So Emile was not mourning for his lost ability. Now, April was left with no choice but to face the inescapable: she had been wrong . . . *and Shirley was right!*

Next week she would leave him. It would be better now than later. She would give him notice, tell him, after their evening out together. But she would have that first. It was a pathetic notion, she knew that, but she wanted to have just one evening out with him. Just one evening spent as if they were an ordinary, uncomplicated couple who were simply enjoying a date.

Surely that wasn't too much to ask?

CHAPTER ELEVEN

'YOU'VE bought us tickets to the opera? April, that's a ridiculous idea. Forget it!'

It was two days after the outing had been mentioned, and they were sitting in the library. Sharkey was playing up again, work was not going well, and April assumed she had just picked the wrong moment to tell Emile of her arrangements.

'You're not backing out of your promise?'

'I promised you nothing,' Emile pointed out. 'You assume too much!'

She couldn't get cross with him; he was right, he hadn't actually made her a promise. 'Why is it a ridiculous idea? If I'd asked you to the ballet I'd be able to see your point. But this is music, Emile. You don't need eyes to enjoy good music. And you do enjoy it, you can't tell me otherwise.'

It was difficult, trying to appear normal, trying to appeal to him logically. 'I thought it would be a lovely evening for us. It'd certainly be a nice change for me.' There it went again, her pride, right out of the window. But she didn't let that stop her. 'I—I've even booked us a private box so we won't disturb anyone if I describe the scenery for you and tell you what everyone's wearing. Please, Emile, do it for me.'

Emile Jacquot sighed inwardly. Do it for her? Dear Lord, he'd do anything in the world for this girl. Anything! He'd tried to resist her, right from the start he'd fought hard to do that. But resisting April was like trying to swim in quicksand.

He knew April Baxter better than she knew herself. She was doing this deliberately, but he wasn't supposed to know that. Ah, what a sweet and precious child she was! She'd walked with him, she'd worked with him and fought with him. She'd talked to him; she'd listened. She'd been his eyes and she'd allowed him, at times, to be hers.

And she'd done it all because she was kindness itself. That, and because she had a tremendous need to be needed.

Her kindness—he had permitted it, accepted it because in the acceptance there was also a giving. And he wanted so much to give to her, to make her happy.

She was happy now. Bless her heart, she would leave Serena House with the knowledge that she had stirred Emile Jacquot to life again. He'd see to that.

Getting him out of the house was her main objective now; no doubt her final one. It was something she'd been leading up to for months. He would go, too. He would give her a memorable evening, and be seen himself to be having the time of his life. For her? Yes, he would do it for her.

April saw his face break into a smile and her heart soared with joy. She'd won! She'd won! 'You'll come out? You will! You were just teasing me, weren't you? The tickets are for Friday, okay? Hey, I'll go and tell Finn. Just think, he'll be able to take a whole evening off!'

Emile broke into laughter. '*I'll* tell Finn. I've just thought of something—the look he'll have on his face when he learns I'm going out. You wouldn't be able to stand it. So I'll tell him!'

It was a memorable evening, a bittersweet evening. April saw it as a tremendous step forward for Emile ... and the close of a very beautiful chapter in her own life.

They dressed up to the nines and April drove Emile's Jaguar into the heart of London. While she couldn't possibly love him any more than she did, she knew an even greater closeness between them this evening, not only because Emile was obliged to take her arm but also because she could tell he was having a wonderful time.

They sat through *The Marriage of Figaro*, an old favourite of them both, each happy with the knowledge that the other was enjoying the show. From time to time April whispered to him, painting for him in words the setting, the scenery, the costumes. They laughed at the silliness of the plot and kept reverently silent as the performers sang their hearts out.

When the show was over, totally unexpectedly Emile announced that he was taking her to supper at the Savoy Hotel.

'The Savoy?' She'd just started the car engine and this came as something of a shock; she'd had her own ideas about what they would do with the rest of the evening. 'Oh, I rather thought——'

Emile looked at her in bewilderment. 'You're disappointed. Why?'

'No, I'm not. Have you booked?'

'Well, no. It isn't necessary at this time of night. April, is something wrong?'

'Not at all!' she said hastily. 'It's just that I thought we could go for a drive, it's such a beautiful warm evening. I—I thought we could sit high on a hill, near home, a hill that overlooks all the twinkling lights of the new town.'

He smiled, a sudden flash of white in the darkly handsome face. 'Ah, to be young! Such impetuosity! But what will we do for food?'

She got enthusiastic then, glad that he was willing to fall in with her plans. 'The chippy! There's a really good fish and chip shop just outside——' She got no further than that. Emile was laughing like a drain.

She dug him playfully in the ribs. 'What on earth's the matter with you? What have I said?' Suddenly she was laughing, not because she understood him but because his own laughter was so infectious.

It was a while before he could speak. April drove off in a fit of the giggles. 'April, I don't believe this. Here I am, offering you a splendid dinner at the Savoy, and you want to sit on a hill eating fish and chips. I don't think I can stand it!'

Her voice was heavily admonitory. 'Emile Jacquot! Don't tell me you've led such an upper-class life that you've never tasted the delightful offerings of an English chippy?'

'Don't be silly. I lived on such things in my student days—the French equivalent, at any rate.'

'Then why are you laughing so much?'

She was half sorry she'd asked that, because he sobered suddenly and she could feel his eyes on her face. 'You don't give a hoot for my wealth, do you?'

'I don't know what you mean.' April was equally serious. 'Do you mean your material wealth?'

Emile's laugh was hollow then. 'What else? I'm virtually a millionaire, my lovely. During my lifetime I've spent as much, too. And here you are buying tickets for a show and offering to buy me supper!'

There was something about his tone that made her feel slightly uneasy. She wondered what was going through his mind. She didn't follow him at all. The conversation had taken a peculiar turn as far as she was concerned and she made an effort to lighten it again, to bring back the laughter.

'Hey, now just a minute! I never said anything about paying for the fish and chips . . .'

It worked. For the time being, at least, Emile became himself again. It was later that she noticed he had grown quiet, subdued.

They were sitting on the hill, enjoying the view in their own different ways, when April felt the urge to ask him what was wrong. But she didn't ask him. She kept her curiosity in check because she was desperate that nothing should happen to spoil this evening.

Emile was in fact many miles away, many years away in his thoughts. Dear God, why was he thinking of Françoise now? Why think of her now, when all he really wanted was to take April in his arms? Physically he was acutely aware of her. Her rose-scented perfume was mingling with the fresh night air, pervading his nostrils, his senses, to the point of intoxication. She was sitting so close to him he could almost see every movement of her head, could almost see her eyes drinking in the sight before them, the twinkling lights. How she enjoyed the simple things! What a beautiful child of nature was April.

He had started to love April long ago, and day by day that love was growing deeper and deeper. But he had no illusions about his love, he knew nothing could come of it. Nothing could ever come of it. It was too late now.

Soon she would leave, never to know she had

plunged him straight into a hell far worse than it ever was before. For how would he survive without her? Reminding himself that he had adjusted once before was no good at all. This was different. Very different.

He had walked into this with his proverbial eyes wide open. There was no one to blame but himself. *Could* he blame himself, for being human? Yes, when he had known what the outcome would be. With his love for April growing every day, his strength was running out. He wanted the impossible: he wanted to spend every minute of the rest of his life with her. He wanted her in every sense of the word. He wanted her so much that he had long ago ceased to touch her in any way. He dared not do that. He simply couldn't trust himself to touch her. There was a limit to what he could take from her. And making love to April would be the ultimate self-indulgence which would make his future hell truly unbearable. He would be lucky to survive as it was.

April stirred beside him, saying something he didn't hear. His thoughts had gone full circle and now, despite himself, he was thinking once more of Françoise. His mouth twisted in annoyance as he thrust the thought away. Damn it, he didn't *want* to think of Françoise! Not now. Not tonight, of all nights . . .

'Come on, April, let's go. It's getting cold.' His voice came out far more sharply than he had intended, and April looked at him in surprise. Where had he been in his thoughts just now? Why had he grown more and more subdued all evening?

'What—what is it, Emile? What's wrong?'

He didn't answer her. As she climbed into the car she felt sick with anxiety. She glanced at him uncertainly. He looked strained, but she waited until they got indoors before she asked him again what was wrong. By then, she had no choice but to ask again. Emile hadn't spoken at all during the last lap of their journey and she was growing frantic at the thought that she might possibly have made some sort of dreadful mistake in coaxing him out of the house. Was there a danger that she'd done quite the wrong thing tonight? In showing him how much enjoyment the world still had to offer, had she succeeded only in reminding him how much was still missing?

'Emile, I—you didn't enjoy this evening, did you?' She almost died at the fleeting expression of pain that crossed his face.

'It was the most wonderful evening I've spent in a long time. I wish I'd done it before, April. I should have listened to you a long time ago. Thank you.'

April's heart plummeted. Emile's words were flat, automatic, insincere. She felt her throat tighten, her hands begin to tremble. Why was he lying to her? What had happened half way through the evening that had made him change so much?

Without thinking, she reached up to touch his face. When he stiffened slightly, his eyes closing against the gesture, she let her hand fall away. She knew, then, that the evening had been a ghastly mistake. She knew also, suddenly, what had been going through his mind. 'You . . . tonight reminded you of something, didn't it? You—you were thinking of your past?'

Emile didn't deny it, nor did he say anything. He just shrugged.

April bit hard on her lower lip, grateful, for once, that he could not see her face, the pain, the silent tears which were shining in her eyes. If she'd needed any confirmation—any *further* confirmation—that

Shirley had been right, she was getting it now. Emile had been thinking about Françoise tonight. 'You—you were thinking about your wife, weren'+ you?'

Emile looked at her sharply, curiously, and April steeled herself, fighting to control the sob rising in her throat. 'Yes,' he said softly, 'as a matter of fact, I was.' He turned away from her then, walking towards the drawing room. 'Come on, let's get ourselves a nightcap. I could use a drink.'

April didn't move. It took every ounce of her willpower to control the near hysteria rising inside her, to force her voice to speak with some semblance of dignity. 'No, thanks, I—I'll call it a day, if you don't mind. I'm rather tired.'

Emile turned around just as she reached the stairs, his eyes narrowing slightly. 'As you wish. Is something wrong, April?'

April gripped the banister for support. Her legs felt as if they were about to give way beneath her. She had to say it—now. Though her heart and her soul cried out against it, she had to tell him she was leaving. 'No. Well, it's just that I've been thinking lately—my booking—the six months are almost up and—well, I know I promised to stay until your book was finished, but . . . That is, we ought to discuss this some time, seeing that you're not even halfway through the novel . . .'

The expression on his face made her voice trail away. Was it disappointment, puzzlement, or what? She had no idea what he was thinking. When he spoke, however, it became painfully obvious that he wasn't disappointed.

'Yes, we must discuss this. Our arrangement was only for six months, and you can't stay here indefinitely. Perhaps we can talk about it tomorrow?'

'No, I—I'm going to my niece's birthday party tomorrow. I won't be back till Sunday.'

He was almost brusque with her then. 'Very well. We'll talk about it on Sunday. Goodnight.'

As soon as the drawing room door closed behind him, April ran up the stairs, the tears coursing down her face.

She flung herself down on the bed, her arms crossed tightly over her stomach as if it would offset the pain inside her. So much for her beautiful evening! Memorable, it certainly would be. Would she ever be able to forget that the one and only time she'd been out with Emile, he'd spent half the evening thinking about the wife he'd lost to another man? The wife he was still in love with.

CHAPTER TWELVE

BEHAVING normally at her niece's birthday party and chatting to Alan and Moira had taxed April to the limit. She made her escape from her brother's home first thing Sunday morning and drove far more quickly than she should have back to Serena House.

But as soon as she came in sight of the tall iron gates she stopped the car. Then she backed away a little, not wanting to attract the attention of the dogs. She told herself she needed a little time to think before she faced Emile.

A hollow laugh escaped from her. Time to think? That was all she had been doing with her spare time for the past several weeks. Nonetheless, her mind was in utter turmoil. For the sake of her own sanity she must leave Emile's employ as soon as possible. But if he wanted her to stay till the end of her booking, another four or five weeks, she would. She had made that agreement at the beginning. Apart from that, she simply wouldn't be able to refuse him, no matter how much pain it cost her.

She reached out to turn on the ignition then immediately switched it off again. Dear Lord, would her mind never stop going round in circles? She cursed her own weakness, her own indecision—her longing not to leave Emile at all.

She buried her face in her hands, feeling the stickiness of perspiration on her forehead. The interior of the car was like an oven and she was feeling lightheaded. What would she say if he asked her to stay for a further six months, until he actually finished his book? What excuse could she give for refusing? There was every chance he would ask this of her; she was, after all, very good at her job. But how could she possibly stay for another six months, loving him as she did, wanting him—and knowing he was still in love with someone else?

Her mind was spinning. She felt as if she were caught between the devil and the deep blue sea, and she forced herself to set the car in motion, fixed in an agony of indecision.

Finn released the gates for her and she let herself in with her front door key. There was no sign of Emile in the drawing room or the library. In the kitchen she saw there was steam coming from the kettle and she assumed that Finn had taken coffee up to Emile's rooms. That was odd. Why was he in his rooms on a beautiful day like today?

She went upstairs, showered and slipped into a pair of shorts and a tee-shirt. No sooner had she finished dressing than Finn knocked on her door. He came in looking disturbed, somewhat baffled.

'What is it, Finn?'

'I don't rightly know, miss. Monsieur Jacquot has been very—er—subdued this last day or so. He spent a lot of time on the phone yesterday and—well, he drank rather more than usual last night.'

'He's probably been thinking about his book. It isn't going at all well, you know.'

Finn nodded. 'Anyway, he knows you're home. He told me to come and ask if you'd go to him. He's in the drawing room now.'

'I—I'll be right down. My hair's wet. I'll just put a comb through it.' Her stomach lurched sickeningly. So Emile wanted to talk to her straight away? He was going to ask her to stay on, to wait till his work was finished . . .

Emile wasn't in the drawing room. He was sitting behind his desk in the library, and April was reminded of the day she had first met him. He was wearing black, as he used to in the early days, and it made her wonder about the mood he was in.

He was distant, too. Not only was the desk a barrier between them, he was distinctly aloof, and the faint smile he gave her as she sat down did nothing to put her at ease.

'Emile . . .?'

There was no beating about the bush. 'April, I have very good news. Very convenient news, that is. Max phoned yesterday and he wants me to go to America with him this Friday. We're taking an afternoon flight to California. We'll be over there for a couple of weeks, having discussions with the screenwriter and director of the film they're making. Of course, I'm not asking you to leave Serena House immediately; mid-week will probably suit you better.' He smiled then, waving a dismissive arm. 'But this has put an end to the discussion we were going to have, hasn't it?'

For as long as she lived, April would never forget the shock of his words. Leave Serena House mid-week? *Mid-week?* Her hand flew to her mouth and all she could think of in that moment was the perversity of human nature. The decision had been taken out of her hands, her brain was telling her this was all for the best, but her heart seemed to have a will of its own.

She just wasn't prepared for this! She'd been counting—she had to face it now—she'd been counting on at least another month with Emile.

'April?'

So far, the moment of leaving had been a vague point in the future, and knowing that had enabled her to hang on to her composure. Now she was actually faced with the *reality* of leaving Emile, everything was crumbling to pieces around her.

'I—C-couldn't I come with you? I mean, I hadn't thought of leaving straight away and . . . and you'll need a secretary——'

'No.' Again there was a dismissive wave of his arm. 'Max is taking his personal secretary. I'm sorry this is short notice, April, but I know it'll be no problem for you to get another job. Morrison's will see you all right.'

She looked at him through a blur of tears, the lump in her throat making speech impossible. How could he tell her like this? How could he be so businesslike? All he was feeling was a slight embarrassment because it was short notice—that was why he was being so aloof! Didn't he care anything at all about her? Had he no idea how much he was hurting her feelings with his— his coolness? This! After five months of friendship—this!

'I—I'll see you when you get back, won't I? Emile, I will see you?' She hadn't meant to say it. She hadn't meant to say anything remotely like that, but her needs were winning over her logic, over her dignity.

'No. This is goodbye, I'm afraid. But I'd like to say——'

'But I could wait for you! I could stay here with Finn . . .'

'Don't be silly. Where I go, Finn goes.'

'But what about the book? We're little more than halfway through it!' If it hadn't been so pathetic, she could have laughed at her own about-face.

Emile reached for a cigarette, his velvet voice as calm as ever. 'You know as well as I do that book's all wrong. I'll have to do a whole rethink, start afresh. I obviously can't say when I'll resume my writing. I need a few weeks' break. I—I don't need the work the way I once used to. You know exactly what I mean by that, don't you?'

Oh, yes, she knew what he meant by that. These days, he wasn't as angry, that was why he didn't need his writing. He wasn't as angry, but he was still wrapped up in memories of Françoise!

April's mind was spinning. She felt very close to fainting. Her hands were trembling and she held them together tightly, almost in an attitude of prayer. 'I—don't understand why you're going to America. You said those people could come here.'

'I know.' He smiled, as if he were proud of himself. 'It's wonderful, isn't it? It's all thanks to you. Leaving the house one week and leaving the country the next!'

April wanted to laugh at the irony of it. So she had at least succeeded in giving Emile a taste for the world outside. For that, a part of her mind would always rejoice. And with his new-found interest he was about to leave the country, leaving her . . .

If only she could go, now, with dignity. If only she could stop these tears and shake him by the hand and wish him well. If only she could be as detached as he was. Surely it was better this way. Better she should never see him again. Never. Surely it was better she should be denied another few weeks with him, weeks which would be as bittersweet as those that had passed.

But logic had no part to play in this, and she broke down then, sobbing quietly, helplessly, wretchedly.

'April, please——' There was a note of surprise in his voice. Coolly he reached into his pocket, handed her his hanky. 'April, why on earth are you so upset?' His tone was softer now. 'I'm very grateful to you, you know. You've been so kind to me these past few months, and I'll never forget——'

'Kind! *Kind?*' Her control deserted her completely and the words came out in an angry burst. 'Emile, I love you! Do you hear me? I love you, and I've loved you for a long time!'

The silence hung in the air between them. She'd said it. It could not be retracted. Furthermore, she didn't give a damn. She didn't care how big a fool she had made of herself. The shock of his announcement, the entire day, the past few weeks—it had all been too much for her, and now the truth was out.

For long seconds Emile Jacquot was motionless. Then he came to her, his eyes closed so that she could not guess his thoughts. Gently he brushed the damp hair away from her face. 'April, my dear April, does your kindness extend so far that you would tell me this? My dear child——'

She brushed his hand away, hating his patronising tone. 'Don't accuse me of that, Emile. You've told me a dozen times how kind I am. Now you're insulting me with it. Allow me to know my own mind. I love you. I love you more than anything in the world. And that has nothing to do with kindness.' Her voice trailed away. It was hopeless. He didn't believe her. Or he refused to believe her. This was his way of keeping detached, keeping her at a distance because he could in no way reciprocate. There was nothing there for him to give. Nothing he could give to *her*.

'April, listen to me. I'm flattered, but this emotion is not real. In time you'll see that it's only an extension of your kindness, your beautiful nature. Don't you see? You have such a tremendous capacity for giving. This was one of the earliest things I learned about you. You've told me about the way you nursed both your parents when they were dying. Then there was that time Alan and the children had 'flu, and the first thing you wanted was to go dashing to them. Why, you even wanted to give up your flat, your career, in order to look after him and his children. Without thought of self you'd have done that. And you'd have had no life of your own.

'You call yourself a realist, but you're romantic in the extreme. I've pointed this out to you a hundred times. You came here and saw in me a man who'd cut himself off from life. You made a determined effort to communicate, to show me how much life still has to offer. Well, you've succeeded, and I shall be eternally grateful to you for that.'

The gentleness in his voice served only to increase the pain in her heart. He was speaking of his gratitude, the last thing she wanted. She said nothing. There was no point in saying anything at all. He was convinced of the truth of his words.

'Your silence says so much. I understand what you're feeling. You think I'm wrong. You think you love me. Believe me, you'll see things differently in a few weeks. My dear, I've lived far longer than you. Soon, you'll see that I'm right, and then everything will fall into the right perspective. You'll look back on your time here and it will be, I hope, a pleasant memory. But it will be no more than that. In time you'll meet someone you'll really love. Please God, it will be someone worthy of you, someone who can offer you a normal life——'

'Emile, I'd like to go now. I really feel it will be better for me to leave straight away. Right now.' April stood, forcing herself to meet the eyes she had learned to read so well. They were bleak, grey, just as they'd been so many times in the past. So he did feel something for her. Not much, but enough that he couldn't hide his sympathy for her. It was unbearable—unbearable and embarrassing for them both.

'Yes, perhaps you're right. That would be best.'

He moved away, and she headed quickly for the door.

'Let me know when you're ready.'

'No! Don't come to me. If you want to make this a little easier then stay in here. Please.'

He nodded slowly, a wry smile pulling at his mouth. 'Goodbye, April.'

'*Au revoir*, Emile.' The finality of goodbye was something she could not bring herself to utter.

Many of her clothes were left unpacked, bundled into her car without care. A numbness had descended on her so that she moved like an automaton. Finn was standing beside her in the garage, uncomfortable and upset. 'That's it, miss. There's nothing else in your room. I—I don't know what's going on, but I'm very sorry to see you like this.'

She forced herself to smile at him. Dear Finn, how fond of him she'd become! 'You're going to America on Friday, that's what's going on. In five days' time you'll be with your master in sunny California. Oh,

Finn, don't look at me like that! He'll explain everything to you.'

'But—you'll come back, won't you? When we get home?'

'No. Emile isn't going to finish his book. At least, not just yet. He—Goodbye, Finn.' She flung her arms around the broad neck, reached up to kiss the florid cheek. 'Take care!'

She climbed into the driver's seat and wound her window down. 'Finn, you have my address—if there's ever . . . if you ever think I might . . . I mean, if the Count——' She didn't know what she wanted to say, but Finn did.

'I will, miss.' Then, in a few little words which said it all, 'I know how you feel.' He watched her as she drove away, bewildered by this sudden turn of events. Then he went briskly indoors to talk to the boss, anxious to find out what was really going on.

CHAPTER THIRTEEN

AT midnight April was still wearing her shorts and tee-shirt, sitting in the kitchen of her flat nursing a cup of coffee which had long since grown cold. She did not remember making it. She didn't remember driving from Buckinghamshire to Paddington. But she did remember every word that had passed between herself and Emile that afternoon. Every last word.

Her sense of rejection was unlike anything she had ever experienced. The man who was the centre of her life had gone from it, as easily and detachedly as he had allowed her into his world. With so little emotion, leaving her with a heart which ached with love for him. That, and his gratitude.

How could he put her love down to kindness? A man such as he, with such an enormous capacity for understanding human emotions, how could he confuse the two? Maybe he hadn't. Maybe that had just been his way of avoiding further embarrassment.

Stiff from sitting so long in one position, April forced herself to walk into the living room. The first thing she saw was her reproduction of Jacquot's 'Orchard in Versailles'. On the sofa were the clothes she had thrown there earlier. She pushed them on to the floor and sat down again, unable to make herself get undressed, unable to take her eyes from the painting.

It was turned three in the morning when she finally

went to bed. She made no entry in her diary; she had written nothing in it since the day she and Emile had talked about Jacquot, the day she had been forced to accept that Shirley had been right all along. And what could she write in it now? What would she be able to write in the future, when without Emile there was no future?

April woke up at five. After nearly six months of early rising her internal clock would take a while to adjust to normal hours. Her eyes flew open from a restless, dreamless sleep. As she realised she was not at home but in her flat, panic took hold of her. The quietness of the room was loud against her ears and within seconds her bewildered mind was filled with questions.

What had she done wrong that Emile didn't even *ask* her to stay on? He was only going to be in California for two weeks, he'd said, so why not even ask her to resume her stay when he returned? It wasn't as if he'd been afraid she might embarrass him with further declarations, because she hadn't told him how she felt at that point.

Yes, human nature was perverse indeed. Or maybe it was just that people in love can behave totally illogically. Whatever, all she knew then was the deepest regret that she had told Emile she wanted to have a discussion about her booking. If only she hadn't said that, about leaving, maybe he would have kept her on, maybe she'd be with him now.

She got out of bed feeling as tired as she had when she'd got into it. In the kitchen she splashed cold water on to her face and half closed the blinds, unable to bear the brilliance of the morning sun. By lunchtime she finally got round to bathing, only to slip her housecoat back on and sit down again, staring into space.

What hurt more than anything was the feeling of total rejection. She felt as if she were good for nothing, for no one. She would never get over the way Emile had dismissed her, in every sense of the word, so coolly. The confidence she had lacked as a woman had grown during her months with Emile—only to be smashed to bits by his treatment of her. All her mental schooling, all her common sense had not prepared her for that.

But of course it hadn't. Who had she been trying to kid all those months? One could only fool oneself for so long, if at all. Of course she'd hoped for a future with Emile. Despite everything that stood against her, she had hoped. She was only human. How could one love so deeply without wishing, hoping some love would be returned? Some . . . just some . . .

Wednesday found her sitting on the settee, still unable to find a good reason for getting dressed. She'd been living on tea and toast, and the clothes she'd pushed on to the floor days ago were still lying there. She felt physically and mentally exhausted. Nobody phoned, and April made no effort to get in touch with the world outside. She hadn't even phoned her agency; work would be impossible. She couldn't work when all she really wanted to do was to curl up and die. If her life had been empty before meeting Emile, it was totally barren now. For April there would never be anyone else. There was no one like Emile. He was everything she wanted and respected in a man. And she was very hard to please.

It was odd, really. She had given so much thought to the day—that vague point in the future—when she would have to leave Serena House, but she had given no thought at all as to what life would actually be like without Emile, what even a few days would be like without seeing him.

Some commonsense part of her mind—or perhaps it was a basic instinct for survival—was still telling her everything had happened for the best. That it was better to have one sharp shock than days and days of pain. But the voice in her head did not console her; she didn't even believe it.

She still wasn't sleeping. At a little after midnight that evening she did something she had never done before. She ventured outside and walked the streets for two solid hours, oblivious to possible dangers. She wasn't trying to tire out her body, she was trying to still her mind, to stop it going round and round in useless circles, to stop herself from saying 'If only, if only . . .'

On Friday morning the trilling of the telephone brought April out of a half doze. She raced to answer it with her heart hammering against her ribs. This was the day Emile was due to leave for California. Could this be him? Was there a chance he'd changed his mind about taking her back when he returned?

Before she had even reached the phone she checked herself. It wouldn't be Emile. Even if he wanted to, he wouldn't ask her back now she'd made a fool of herself and embarrassed him with a declaration of love, like some lovesick teenager.

It was Alan. 'April, what's happening? I phoned Serena House last night and that chap with the gruff voice told me you weren't working there any more.

What's going on? Has you-know-who finished the book?'

'Yes. It's finished. The job's come to its natural conclusion.' She shocked herself with her lie, but it was the only way she could handle things just now. Later she would have to tell Alan about the unfinished book, but he would never know what had really happened. As much as April was desperate to talk to someone, Alan would be the last person capable of understanding.

How she longed for someone to talk to, though! If only Shirley were here. But Shirley was two hundred miles away now and the last thing she would need was an hysterical phone call from April only days after she'd returned from her honeymoon.

April said not a word to Alan; she just kept quiet and let him ramble on. As she listened, she caught sight of herself in the hall mirror. She looked ghastly. Under her eyes there were dark circles. Her hair was unwashed, uncombed. She looked ill. She felt ill.

'I'd like to see you this weekend,' Alan said.

'What? Oh—no, I'm not coming this weekend. To be honest, I—I'm not feeling too well. I couldn't cope with the children.'

Alan's voice took on confidential tones. 'I don't want you to come here, Sis. I want to come and see you. There's—there's something I want to tell you.'

April cast a curious look at the telephone receiver. 'Well, all right. I mean, of course you can come.' Dear Lord, she had to get a grip on herself. She didn't want Alan guessing something was wrong. Something was wrong? How was she going to hide from him the fact that her world had fallen to pieces?

'Tomorrow afternoon?'

'Yes. Yes, Alan. Any time.'

After putting the receiver down she forced herself to tidy up a little. At all costs she must make an effort. She didn't want her brother to find her looking like death warmed up, with the flat in turmoil. She didn't want him to know of her heartbreak. Since the day he had accused her of falling in love with Emile, April had mentioned the Count only in the most casual way and as infrequently as possible. She had answered Alan's questions about her work but had volunteered almost nothing about how well she and Emile were getting on in their off duty hours, because she had never got over her disgust at Alan's warning not to fall in love with a blind man, and any deeper discussion of the relationship would have caused a further, pointless argument.

At a little before noon she walked to the corner shop to pick up coffee and bread. Afterwards she went into the little park a few streets from her flat. It was a warm day and the sky was a perfect blue, heralding the start of an Indian summer. April closed her eyes, imagining the grounds of Serena House, how splendid and breathtakingly beautiful they would be when the leaves changed into their autumn colours.

As she rounded the corner on her way home she saw a taxi parked outside the entrance to the flats. She made no haste, not thinking for one moment that someone was visiting her. When she got to the main door she saw a huge parcel leaning against the wall, and a taxi driver with his finger on her doorbell. It was seconds before she could find her voice. 'Is—is that for me?'

The driver looked relieved. 'You're Miss Baxter?

Yes. And this.' He thrust a small parcel into her hands, offering to carry the big parcel inside for her.

'Th-thank you. Yes, I'm on the first floor. If you'll follow me.' She opened the door with trembling hands, her mind spinning in confusion. She knew what was inside the big parcel, just as she knew she'd never be able to carry it without assistance. It had been very well wrapped, but its shape could not be disguised.

The taxi driver leaned it against the wall of her living room. April tipped him, thanked him, put her shopping bag and the small package on the floor and stood, staring at the wrapped painting in disbelief.

Why? Why had Emile done this? What could he be thinking about, sending her an original painting worth thousands of pounds? Was this further evidence of his gratitude, gratitude she didn't want? And what of himself, why had he sent her one of his four remaining paintings after he'd told her they were in Serena House solely for his pleasure?

She dropped to her knees and tore a small strip in the brown paper. Beneath that there was corrugated cardboard, and she poked a hole through it, just big enough so that she could satisfy her curiosity and see which painting it was. She had no intention of unwrapping it. She would not be keeping it. She couldn't possibly do that.

It was the painting from over the fireplace in the library, the one she had enjoyed day after day for the past five months. The one by which she had first had her memory jogged when she had recognised the Count as being Jacquot.

She looked at her watch. There had to be an

explanation for this, and Emile had presented her with a perfect excuse to phone him.

But it was too late. There was, as she'd expected, no reply from Serena House. Its occupants were probably winging their way to America by now. But of course, Emile had not intended to let her phone. He had timed this delivery purposely, knowing he would be gone by the time the taxi driver got to London. He didn't want to speak to her. He wouldn't want any further scenes. This painting was just a gift, and she must read nothing more into it than that.

There was, however, more to it than that. When April remembered the small package she opened it uninterestedly, thinking it was some small item she'd left in her bedroom. Not that she'd noticed anything was missing. But then she wouldn't have; she hadn't put everything away yet.

It was a cassette. At first she looked at it stupidly, knowing it wasn't one of hers because it was unmarked, but at a loss to understand its significance. Then she moved like lightning, fetching her tape recorder and fumbling to insert the cassette with hands which were suddenly trembling.

A few seconds later Emile's dark brown velvet voice was speaking to her as clearly as if he were sitting beside her. 'Hello, April. I'm sending you this painting because I know how much you like it. It's yours to do with as you wish. I hope you'll regard it as a house guest, as I did, but whether you keep it for a year or for a lifetime I know you'll eventually see that it's passed on to a suitable recipient. The other three paintings have been packed up and sent to the gallery where my first British exhibition was held. I'm ready to let them go, and I know this will please you.'

There was a pause, and when next he spoke his accent was very slightly more pronounced, even though the words came more slowly. 'You'll realise now that I took note of your remarks when we first discussed Jacquot. I had the feeling you didn't believe me when I said I had let go of the past—so here's my proof. There are so many other things in life from which I now get pleasure, and it's all thanks to you. Goodbye, April. Remember me from time to time.'

For the first time since leaving him, April wept. Great convulsive sobs took control of her, leaving her body drained of energy. So Emile really was a happier man these days; at least, his heart had melted sufficiently that he had taken the trouble to send her a gift.

April sat on the floor, playing the tape over and over again. It was her turn, now, to make an adjustment. She too must face the future. A future without Emile. He didn't need her any longer and she must let go emotionally. She must not think of self, of her own heartache. She must be thankful she'd managed to do something, however little, for Emile Jacquot. Maybe, given more time, he would even start to get over Françoise.

CHAPTER FOURTEEN

IN the early hours of the following morning April woke to find herself soaked in perspiration. She'd had a very disturbing dream. Nothing actually unpleasant had happened in it; she kept seeing Emile in all his different moods, sitting at the piano with her, laughing while she sang. Then there was the vision of him sitting, shrouded in an aura of cold desolation, in the garden. Then she was sitting with him in the library, taking dictation—and the next minute she could feel his gentle touch upon her face when he had looked at her for the first time.

The dream left her disturbed, frightened.

She spent the morning cleaning. Cleaning frantically, almost desperately, as if she would thus exorcise every memory of every minute in Serena House. Perhaps, when she was thoroughly physically exhausted, she would somehow be renewed.

Alan came in the afternoon. If she'd managed to live through a couple of weeks without seeing her brother, she would have managed to maintain her composure. But the wound was too new, the adjustment barely under way, and all she wanted to hide from him was etched only too plainly on her face.

'Good grief, you look awful!' Such was Alan's greeting when she opened the door to him.

'It's just a cold,' she smiled. 'They say summer colds are the worst, don't they?'

Alan followed her through to the kitchen. 'But

you've lost weight, April. Have you been really ill? Why didn't you let me know? I thought you were sickening for something last weekend, you were so quiet . . .'

'Don't fuss.' She forced herself to smile at him. 'If I've lost weight then it was worth it. Tea or coffee?'

'What's that big package in the living room? Oh, tea, please.'

April turned away from him, busying herself with teacups and things. 'You don't miss much, do you? It's—it's a sort of bonus for a job well done. From Jacquot.'

'You mean it's one of *his*? Heavens, it must be worth a fortune! You can't possibly accept it, April.'

'I know that,' she said shortly. 'Bring the tray through, will you? And change the subject. You're here to tell me your news, remember?'

'But I don't get it. A bonus, you say? You don't give someone a bonus worth thousands of pounds, not something like *that*, no matter how efficient they've been! What gives?'

April walked ahead of him, telling herself he was only being naturally curious. The trouble was that she didn't know how to answer him.

'Perhaps the Count has more money than he has sense.' She shrugged. 'But of course I shall send it back.' She thought he would let it go at that, that she'd given the sort of answer which would satisfy him.

Alan didn't say anything else, but he obviously wasn't satisfied with her answer. He looked at her hard and long, as if she had insulted his intelligence. But he at least had the tact not to press her any further, and April felt a rush of gratitude. Her nerves were stretched to breaking point at it was.

'So what have you got to tell me?' She smiled as his face broke into a grin. She hadn't seen him looking so relaxed in a long time.

'Can't you guess?'

'I'm just beginning to get an inkling now.' Then she was really smiling. 'Would it be something to do with you and Moira?'

Alan pulled his pipe from his pocket, still grinning, then he flung his jacket over the back of the chair. 'I've asked her to marry me.'

'Oh! Alan, that's—well, it is a surprise! That's pretty quick, isn't it?'

'No! She's been with me almost five months, and you can get to know someone very well in five months. Especially when you live under the same roof.'

Five months! But of course it was five months. How the time had flown . . . and yes, one ought to know someone well, if one had been living with them for so long. One *ought* to . . .

'It just happened, Sis,' Alan went on. 'I liked her right from the start, but you know that. You wouldn't believe how well we get on. We're so compatible! We've got so much in common. And the kids adore her. Are you happy for me, April? Please say you are!'

'Oh, darling, of course I am! I wish you all the happiness in the world, you know that. It's wonderful news! I'll phone Moira later, to congratulate her. I'm delighted, Alan.' So she was. For Alan she was very happy; she'd wanted him to remarry, and Moira was a very likeable woman.

Alan came over and hugged her then. 'Oh, April, you're such a kind person.'

Instantly the tears started prickling at the back of her eyes. What a thing for him to say—now, when it was the last thing she wanted to be told.

'I'm sick of hearing that. From you and . . . and from other people. Besides, it's uncalled-for and silly. What other reaction had you expected from me?'

Alan went back to his seat, tapped out his pipe and avoided her eyes as he started filling it. 'I knew you'd be pleased. But you had a perfect opportunity there to get back at me for my stupid and thoughtless reaction when you told me you'd fallen in love with the Count. You didn't take it, and that's why you're kind.'

'I never told you I was in love with the Count.'

He met her eyes then. 'You didn't need to. Just as you don't need to tell me now that something awful has happened. I hope you will tell me, though. Share it with me, April. Don't give me any more of this rubbish about having a summer cold.'

April started crying as she started talking. The invitation to share her troubles with her brother was more than she could resist. She didn't expect him to understand, even though love had come into his life and taken him by surprise. Nor did she tell him everything. But Alan listened intently. He didn't hurry her and he didn't interrupt until she was weeping so much that she could no longer talk. Then he asked questions and more questions, like the solicitor that he was, as if he were weighing the evidence. When he made his pronouncement on the case he shook his sister to the core.

'I can't accuse you of stupidity, April, because stupid is one thing you're not. It's simply that you're so close to the situation you're unable to view it objectively. I'd say not only does Emile Jacquot feel as you do, he loves you so much that he's made the ultimate sacrifice—letting you go.'

There was, naturally, a split second during which she believed him. Because she wanted to. And because Alan was saying it. And Alan was very sensible and logical. But common sense returned rapidly. 'What are you talking about? How on earth do you reach that conclusion?'

Her voice had risen to a very high pitch, but Alan spoke quietly, shrugging as if it were all crystal clear to him. 'From a dozen things you've told me. The Count trusted and respected you, that much you can surely see for yourself. Slowly your relationship grew despite the fact that he fought against it. You've just said you had that impression yourself, that he was resisting you every inch of the way. Don't you see *why*? Can't you see now *why* he cut you out of his life?'

'Alan, there's something you don't understand——'

'Because he's blind, April. He's *blind*!'

April was on her feet, furious and disappointed. 'That's sheer and utter rubbish! You're letting your own bias colour your thinking. I don't care that he's blind! And Emile knows that. We had *that* sorted out right from day one!'

'Now I do think you're stupid.' Alan leaned back in his chair in an infuriatingly cool manner, lighting his pipe slowly, as if in a few more seconds April would understand everything.

'I want you to go now, Alan. I'm very tired, and frankly you're the last person in the world to understand a situation such as this.'

'Sit down and shut up!' He got up suddenly, half pushing her back on to the settee. It had been a long, long time since she'd seen him annoyed like this, and she could only conclude that she'd really hurt his feelings.

'In case you didn't understand me earlier, I've apologised for my remarks about Emile's handicap. I know, now, that when you fall in love with someone you don't stop to examine their imperfections. Moira is five years older than I. She's from an entirely different background and she's very poorly educated. And I've recently learned that she wasn't widowed when her son was three, she was abandoned by her lover when she discovered she was pregnant. She's never been married. But do you think for one minute that it makes me feel any differently about her? That I'd have changed my mind because her past isn't impeccable? I love what she is, just as you love Emile—with or without his sight. I'm learning, you see? And I'm not really the insensitive brute you take me for. I know Emile's blindness makes no difference to you. But it makes a difference to *him*.'

April looked at him in astonishment. For Alan, that was quite an outburst. Maybe he had learned a few things. Moira must have influenced him more than she thought, and that was all to the good.

Her anger died away as quickly as it flared up. Alan was trying to understand, and for that she was grateful. But he'd got it all wrong. 'There's something you don't understand. I—Emile and I were friends, that's all. You see, he . . . he's still in love with his wife.'

Alan looked at her as if she were talking gibberish. 'Is that what he told you? And you swallowed it? Don't you see he's just trying to——'

'No, no.' April waved an impatient hand. 'He didn't tell me—he didn't need to. It's the truth, Alan. I should have seen it a long time ago, when Shirley first mentioned it, in fact. But I'd reached my own conclusions and I——'

'Shirley?' he frowned. 'Are you telling me this is Shirley's opinion?'

'Well—originally, yes. But it's obvious when you think about it. You see——' She broke off, sighing deeply. 'Oh, Alan, there's so much you don't know . . .'

'So tell me,' Alan said simply. 'I've got all the time in the world. I'm going to sort this out, April. Come on, surely you can confide in your brother?' When she said nothing, he pressed harder. 'Please trust me, Sis. I will understand, you know. Tell me everything. Tell me all the bits you omitted the first time round.'

April talked for more than two hours. She went right back to the beginning and told him everything, all the conclusions she'd reached about Emile mourning for his art—and how he'd convinced her she was wrong. Everything.

When she had finally finished she looked up to find Alan smiling at her patiently. 'It's as clear as the nose on your face, my dear. The trouble is you just can't see straight. Think about it now. Think of the difference between the man you've just described to me compared with the man you first told me about. Look at the difference. Can't you see how much you've influenced his life?'

'Well, yes, but Shirley——'

'Shirley is wrong. Just as you were wrong.'

'But the night we went to the opera . . . Emile admitted he'd been thinking about Françoise.'

'So what?' Alan laughed hollowly. 'That's bound to happen from time to time. It could have been anything—just one little thing—that reminded him of her. Maybe it was someone's perfume, or something you said, or perhaps the music. Things like that happen all the time. Do you think a day goes by when I'm not reminded of Liz? Besides, you've no evidence to show that Emile was enjoying his memories. You said he became almost morose.'

'Yes, but surely——'

'Look, April. Emile has sent you away because he's blind, I tell you. Think of it practically: he's years older than you, then there's the consideration of children—how would he cope with children around him? A young wife would want them, that's for sure. Don't you see he's afraid because there are so many things he wouldn't be able to share with you? He's let you go for your own sake!'

'No...' April's voice was barely audible because she daren't allow herself to think there was some truth in all this, some hope. 'No. You're barking up the wrong tree! I've told you how efficient Emile is. He's got everything in that house paced out to perfection. He would be able to cope with children. Even ... even if I've got it wrong about his ex-wife, he still doesn't love *me*. And he doesn't even believe that I love him! We've got to face facts!'

Alan shook his head, looking at her with a mixture of impatience and pity. That, and a great deal of love. 'Your main trouble is that you can't believe how easy it is to love you, how very special you are. You can't believe Emile would love a so-called plain girl like you. He loves you, all right. And since we're finally dealing with *facts* instead of theories, consider this: your kindness is a fact, and Emile knows as much about that as I do. Don't you see he couldn't ask you to stay with him or return to him later—when he thinks you'd accept out of kindness?'

April reached for a cigarette, her hands trembling and her mind whirling in confusion. 'But he *knows* his blindness makes no difference to me!'

'Does he?' Alan said quietly, getting to his feet. 'Does he really? I'm going now. I'll leave you to think about all this. For heaven's sake, don't start weeping again!' He laughed then, derisively. And it was quite deliberate, because he wanted to press home a point. 'You talk about this lovely rapport you had with Emile. Ha! It seems to me you've spent too much time playing the piano and strolling under the moon—and you haven't got down to basic communication. Get back to Serena House and *communicate*, April. Try using good-old fashioned words. It won't happen by telepathy!'

He sounded like his old self again, but there was no denying that there was a lot of truth in what he said. At the door, he slipped an arm around April's shoulders. 'I like the sound of Emile Jacquot, for what it's worth. And the sooner you come to your senses, the sooner I'll be able to welcome him as my brother-in-law.'

'Wh-what do you mean?'

April's brother looked heavenward, hooked his jacket over his shoulder and stuck his pipe between his teeth. 'Just this: when I first told Moira I loved her, she smiled sadly, told me not to confuse love with my gratitude towards her for all she'd done for me and the children. Did I offer her a job for five years as a way of proving my love? No, I proved it in the only way I could, and you've heard about that today.'

He looked down at her, smiled, nodded and left.

As the days passed, April alternated between believing her brother and thinking him idiotically optimistic because everything in his world was rosy and he thought everything in April's world could be made that way, too. Her moods shifted accordingly from elation to depression.

Alan had gone up in her estimation. He had listened and he had understood. Over and over again she weighed all the facts, as Alan's legal mind had sifted them. Still, she ended up getting nowhere.

It was true that she didn't have any actual evidence about Françoise—except that Emile had never mentioned her prior to the night of the opera, and that was almost certainly because it must hurt him to speak of her.

As for his blindness ... Why, it was her easy handling of it that had got her the job in the first place!

Finally, there was nothing to show that Emile loved her. Nothing. If there'd been something, just a sign, she would have acted on her brother's advice and gone to talk with Emile.

April was by no means a quitter. Especially when her life was at stake. But how could she go back to Serena House as it was? How could she call on Emile when she had not the slightest encouragement to show there was some hope? She would only cause herself more pain—and Emile a great deal more embarrassment.

Emile had been away for more than a week before April finally unwrapped the painting. Oh, she still had every intention of sending it back, but Emile had sent it as a house guest, and one evening, in a state of severe depression, she unpacked it in the hope that it might give a little comfort. She might just as well enjoy it for the next few days.

There was no tidy way of removing the wrappings, they had been very securely sealed. By Finn, no doubt. April tore at the brown paper very clumsily and then very carefully she slit open the corrugated cardboard with a knife.

A single sheet of paper had been placed between the cardboard and the painting itself. She might have screwed it up without thinking had it not fallen out and landed face upwards on the floor. She looked at it stupidly, uncomprehending. On it there were just two sentences, written in Finn's bold hand: 'Miss, we're not going to America—we're going to Switzerland.'

Switzerland? The eye specialist! Emile had gone to see the Professor!

'. . . He's doing it for you, miss, only for you. Finn.'

April stared incredulously at the last sentence, her whole body trembling so that the note slipped from her hands. Alan's words were ringing in her ears. Dear God, Alan was right! He was *right*! How stupid she'd been, how incredibly stupid! She'd been too busy looking for the complex to see that which was blatantly, glaringly obvious!

It had been obvious to Alan. Obvious, simple and straightforward. Emile did love her! There was no other reason he'd taken his chance with the Professor. '. . . He's doing it for you, miss . . .'

Without any shadow of doubt he loved her as much as she loved him. As much as Alan said he did. Finn knew it, too. April was the last to realise!

She leapt to her feet, snatching at the note and holding it to her breast as her heart sang with joy. Her mind snapped into action and she was able to see everything, for the first time, with total clarity.

There'd been so much evidence to show her Emile *himself* was inhibited by his blindness. Not because he could no longer paint but because he thought he could not allow himself to love or accept love. There had been so many things she had heard but failed to register because she had been fixed with the wrong ideas.

She could hear Emile's voice now, when he had been answering her questions that time when they had talked about Jacquot. 'For the ability to paint,' he had said, 'my heart no longer aches.' She had been so preoccupied with her own theories that she hadn't stopped to think about the way he had qualified his answer.

And he had said, 'It's gone now, and I accept that totally and completely. I only wish that other people would accept it, too.'

A wave of shame engulfed her as she thought of that last sentence, as she looked at the entire situation from Emile's point of view. He knew she had set out to change him. She had spent five months doing just that. No wonder he thought she didn't accept him as he was!

She flew into the hall, snatched up the phone and dialled the number of Serena House. There was no reply, of course. Emile had only been away a little over a week, and heaven knew how long he would be in Switzerland.

Sleep was impossible for April that night. One moment she was smiling from sheer happiness and the next moment she was filled with pain as she realised how little she had understood Emile, after all.

Whenever she got close to sleep, the memory of her last few minutes with him came back to haunt her. 'In time you'll meet someone you really love. Please God, it will be someone worthy of you. Someone who can offer you a normal life.'

A normal life. There would be no question of kindness entering into it if a girl accepted a proposal from a man who could offer a 'normal' life. This trip to Switzerland was Emile's last-ditch, desperate attempt to bring this about. It was something he had to try. The saddest thing of all was that it wouldn't work—and he knew it. Finn's words came drifting to her . . . 'The hospital in London told him categorically there was no hope . . . He said it's something he *knows*, deep down inside, that he'll be blind for the rest of his life.' `

April understood that. People did *know* things from time to time. Inexplicably, but accurately and indisputably. She respected this sort of sixth sense.

No, the professor in Switzerland would not be able to restore Emile's sight. And Emile would never, ever come to her blind. No wonder he had finished with her the way he did—so finally and without as much as a promise. The visit to the Professor was something he had to try, even though he knew it wouldn't work. Oh, how dreadful he must be feeling now, how desperate!

Seventeen more days passed before April got a reply from Serena House. Seventeen dreadful, agonising days and nights of waiting. Days of walking aimlessly through the park, through the streets; nights of restlessness, disturbing dreams, hope, happiness—and worry. The Professor must have operated on Emile, there was no other reason why he should be away so long.

When Finn answered the telephone early one morning, April gently replaced the receiver without speaking. Emile must have no forewarning of her visit, otherwise she might not get past the gates.

She bathed and dressed very carefully, needing every ounce of confidence she could give herself. Would she be able to communicate with Emile, to get through to him? How far inside himself had his experience in Switzerland driven him? Above all, she must be careful not to let him know she realised where he had been. Otherwise it would be hopeless—he would think she was coming to him out of pity.

April did not drive there quickly. She was too nervous to risk that. In fact, nervous was putting it mildly. It wasn't every day that she asked a man to marry her.

Approaching Serena House was something she had done a hundred times, but never before like this, never with such an objective in mind! The Alsatians were there; one of the gardeners was in sight, and the grounds and the trees looked as beautiful as ever in this, the start of autumn, the start of a new season.

Finn was expecting her. Finn was no fool! With his gruff voice he answered the intercom in the nearest he could manage to a whisper, which told her Emile was up and about.

She found the front door open, with Finn waiting just inside the hallway. There was no time to talk, because Emile would have heard the car. Finn took one look at her face and shook his head. 'If things had turned out differently, miss, he'd have come to you.'

'I know,' she whispered. 'Thank you, Finn. Thank you for everything.'

Finn looked hastily towards the drawing room door. 'I—I ought to announce you,' he said half-heartedly. But he stayed right where he was and let her make her own way. At the door April paused, turning to look at him helplessly. He smiled and nodded, in just the same manner Alan had done almost three weeks earlier.

April drew a deep breath, said a silent prayer, and gently opened the drawing room door.

CHAPTER FIFTEEN

THE room was cold despite the fire burning in the grate and there was an atmosphere about it that April didn't care to name.

Emile was sitting in his armchair, eyes closed, his head resting against one of the wings. His lean fingers were curled around an empty brandy glass. He was wearing the clothes he had worn when he had said goodbye, and April's heart constricted at the sight of him. His hair looked greyer at the sides, his mouth was set, thin-lipped, stamped with the cruelty of what life had presented to him—a cruelty she had unwittingly added to. For a moment, she couldn't move, couldn't speak. He looked thinner, unwell and utterly, utterly desolate.

Emile breathed in deeply. How often this perfume had come to haunt him! How often he had imagined her presence, heard her tinkling laughter. Day after day she was there, in his mind, in his heart.

'What is it, Finn? Why are you hovering?'

'I—I'm hovering because I don't quite know whether I'm welcome,' she said softly.

For a moment he was completely without control. April saw the pain, the pleasure and confusion on his face, the jerking of his body as he came upright in his chair. 'April! What—why are you here?' Then, in a voice not at all reminiscent of velvet, he demanded, 'What the hell do you want?'

She moved towards him slowly, in no way fooled by

his rudeness. So this is how it's going to be, she thought, all his defences are up against me. Is he foolish enough to think he can frighten me away?

'I—I had to see you. We are friends, after all. Please hear me out, Emile. I have a problem.'

She held her breath, seeing the battle going on inside him. 'Emile, please!'

'Very well, sit down. I'll always help you if I'm able to. What's troubling you?' The words were right, but the voice was curt.

She sat on a stool, moving it close to him and perching on it nervously. 'It—it's cold in here. Still, autumn has arrived, so what can we expect? The—the garden's looking beautiful. All the trees are beginning to——'

Emile closed his eyes. 'Get to the point, April. What do you want?'

There had been so much she had wanted to say, so many reassuring things she had wanted to tell him before she led up to her proposal. In her mind she had gone over them a million times during those seventeen dreadful days.

But she had waited too long, he had waited too long, and now all she wanted was to throw herself into his arms and beg him to marry her.

'I said what do you want?' His voice was almost vicious and April's breath caught on a sob as she realised from this that he, too, was fighting for control.

'You,' she said quietly. 'But you know that already. You see, your prophecy was wrong. When I told you I love you, you said I should wait a few weeks, see how differently I felt then. I've waited, and I don't feel any different. Being away from you has made me love you more, if that's possible. I want you, Emile, I can't survive without you. I loved you right from the start, I love you now, and I'll love you for ever.'

She saw his fingers tighten around the glass, his mouth twisting as if he'd been stabbed by pain. 'For ever! Oh, April, people should never dare to speak in such terms. We can never——'

'I'm here to ask you to marry me, Emile.'

He started, shocked to the core. His mouth opened and closed but no words came out. She moved closer to him, slipping her hand into his and making no attempt to stop the tears that were streaming from her eyes.

'Emile, please, I know you love me. I *know* you do. Please . . . marry me. I can't go on without you.'

'Oh, April!' Suddenly she was crushed against him, enveloped in the warm strength of his arms. 'Oh, my darling, I do love you. I love you more than I've ever loved anything or anyone. I love you so much that . . .' He laughed hollowly. 'I love you so much that I can't marry you.'

'But why?' She sobbed, clinging to him desperately. 'Why must you shun the happiness that the future can hold? I was made for you, my darling, I think you know that. I've waited for you for a long time. You're all I ever wanted in a man. And you . . . Darling, I think if we'd met in a different place in a different time we wouldn't have loved. But we're here, now, the people we are today, needing each other, wanting each other, and all . . . all you've been through has made you into the man you are today, the man I love. In you there's just a little bit of Jason Jordan, quite a lot of Jacquot—the sensitivity of Jacquot—but mainly you are yourself. Emile. And that's who I love.

'If I'd met you when you were Jacquot I wouldn't have loved you. If I'd met you in ten years' time when you were embittered, wholly Jason Jordan, I wouldn't have loved you. But this is us, now, and in the future we can grow and change together, in the right way.'

'No,' he said quietly. 'That's just where you're wrong. You see, it's—it is Jacquot you love.'

'No!' she cried. 'That's unfair!' She looked at him incredulously and a sudden fear clutched at her heart. A new fear, born of a sudden realisation. 'Who are you confusing me with?' she said slowly. 'Your ex-wife? Is that it, Emile, is that it? I . . . I know about the divorce. It was in the papers. I know about her and—and that other man. What happened? You've never spoken about it. Please tell me! Please tell me now!'

He moved her gently away from him. He got to his feet, lit a cigarette. April waited, knowing that what he was about to tell her was of paramount importance.

'There's not much to tell. I—she—Françoise was my model. One among many. She was incredibly beautiful and I—I was young enough to think beauty was more than skin deep. I found her charming, exciting, bubbling with a zest for living. She came from a poor family. She was intelligent, but her beauty was her main asset, and she knew it. She led me a dance in the beginning. I was crazy about her then, and she knew that, too.

'When we married she changed overnight. Only then did I see her in her true colours. She was in love with money, with the title she inherited when we married, with the kudos of being the wife of . . . I never wanted to be in the limelight. You see, I always liked the quiet life, I always preferred to keep very much behind the scenes, just getting on with my work.

Françoise didn't like that about me. She was always talking to the press, to people in the art world, arranging parties and exhibitions. Exhibitions I didn't actually need—or want. I—I wouldn't . . .'

His voice trailed away. He drew deeply on his cigarette, leaning against the wall as if these memories had exhausted him emotionally.

'You still loved her when you divorced?'

'Yes and no. I'd always understood her and I tried very hard to overlook the way she . . . It wouldn't have lasted, anyway. It would only have been a matter of time before I'd ended up hating the girl. April, I find it very difficult to speak of Françoise to you. She wouldn't have been fit to clean your shoes, my darling. I'm ashamed to think . . . What I felt for her was not real. It wasn't love. I didn't know what love was in those days——'

'But what happened? How did the divorce come about if you still felt something for her? Was it because of this other man?'

'No. She hadn't even met him then. It was nothing so obvious.' His mouth twisted into a wry smile. 'Françoise had a solicitor drawing up divorce papers two weeks after my plane crash. She didn't even wait till I'd left hospital before she told me of her decision. She made it perfectly plain she'd never be able to live with a blind man.'

April bit down on her lip, trying to stifle a horrified gasp. She would never understand Françoise! To think that Emile had regained consciousness to discover he was blind, that he would never paint again, and then—then his own wife showed him how utterly worthless he'd become. What timing! What vicious, emasculating cruelty!

'She moved out straight away,' Emile went on. 'Within a couple of months she'd taken up with this Italian film director. I don't think for one minute that she loved him, but he could offer her the sort of life she wanted—a constant round of parties, publicity, the frequent mentions in the society columns . . .'

April watched him as his voice trailed away. So, inasmuch as Françoise had stood in the way, Shirley had been right. His ex-wife had been the block . . . and she still was. Emile was turning April down—she was paying for the damage done by another woman!

'But, Emile, I'm not Françoise! Don't you see that I'm different?'

'Different?' Emile came quickly to her, taking her hands into his and lifting them to his lips. 'Oh yes, my darling, you're different!'

'Then why reject me?'

'Oh, April, it isn't rejection. Don't say that. I know what that feels like.'

'It is rejection,' she cried. 'When—when you sent me away you made me feel good for nothing, for no one. Why make me pay for what *she* did? Françoise was never in love with you as a man. But I am! I love you just as you are. Why, *why* do you refuse me?'

He pulled her towards him, his arm encircling her waist as he led her towards the settee. 'Because I'm blind, and that's one thing we can never alter. I'm blind, and I'll be like this for the rest of my life.'

'I know that. But what difference does it make?'

His fingers tightened around hers and he smiled sadly. 'How can you say that?'

'Because it's true! It makes no difference to me. It never did and it never will. Emile, there's something I have to make clear. I—the way I was with you, here, during those months ... I didn't try to change you because I was dissatisfied, I loved you long before you even began to change. I—I did it for your sake. No, that's not true, it was for my sake, too. I couldn't bear to see you cut off from all emotion. I knew you were a man capable of enjoying tremendous pleasure. I knew that because you'd been through such pain and—well, pleasure and pain come from the same source. You have a tremendous capacity for loving, for understanding, for living. I did it all because I love you. Love came first. Love me, Emile. Understand me. Live with me as your wife. Accept me. I'll make you happy—I know I can do that.'

He sighed, turning away as though he could see the unhappiness that he knew would be reflected in her eyes. 'April, you just don't seem to understand. Oh, you coped beautifully with my blindness for a few months. But it would be so different in the long term. You're young, you want a normal life, a husband who can share everything with you.'

'But you can. You can! We've proved that already!'

'Darling, there's something I want you to know. I— I didn't go to America ...'

'But—haven't you been away? You mean——'

'... There was ... just the slightest chance that I might be helped. It was a very slim chance, but I took it. I had to try ... I was desperate when you talked about leaving, when I thought I was about to lose you for ever. Had it worked, believe me I'd have been dashing to your door and begging you to marry me. But it didn't work. I—I saw this man in Switzerland. He's an eye specialist, an old friend of the family. I— I'd thought perhaps ... Well, he contacted me some time ago and asked to examine me. He made no promises, but I thought there might be some new technique, new advances over the past few years, and maybe . . .'

'You went to see the Professor?' The incredulity in April's voice was not wholly false. She was surprised Emile was telling her this and in split seconds she made a decision. Here, now, was her chance finally to get through to him. She was fighting for her life.

'Professor?' The word brought his head up sharply. 'You—you *knew* about him?'

'But of course I did. I knew ages ago.' She made her voice light, casual. 'It was one day—I just happened to ask Finn what had happened to the original of "Orchard in Versailles"—you know I always favoured that one. Anyway, Finn told me where it was, about how you'd sent it when you had this contact from your family friend. But so what?'

Jet black eyes were looking at her incredulously. 'You mean you *knew* a chance existed and—and you never mentioned it? Never once did you mention it! There *was* a chance—and you never mentioned it! Why, why?'

April's heart lifted with joy, with the victory she knew was hers. All she had to do was to give him the right answer. 'You once told me you knew you'd be blind for the rest of your life. I accepted that. I understand—I respect this sort of inner knowledge we have at times.' She threw her arms around him. 'You see, darling? Your blindness has never, ever made the slightest difference to me. Now, will you marry me?'

'April!' Emile couldn't say anything else. He didn't want to say anything else. He pulled her into his arms and told her without words how much he loved her.

As his lips came down to hers April felt moisture on

her cheeks. Whether it came from her eyes or Emile's she couldn't say. His lips melted against hers in a kiss that went on and gently on. Then, with a passion which had been too long held in check, his lips became demanding, probing, thrilling. They were kissing as if there were no tomorrow even as they both realised, now, there were so many tomorrows.

When at last he pulled away from her his voice was thick with desire. 'Oh, my darling, if you knew how much I've wanted you! How I've fought to keep——'

'I do know,' she smiled. 'Because I feel exactly the same.' She took his hand, cupping it against the softness of her breast. 'And this will be yet another world you open up for me. Something else you'll introduce me to that's very, very beautiful.'

He cradled her against him, laughing softly because he had found the one he'd waited for—not just for five years, but for all his life. 'This is all wrong, you know. I should be down on my knees begging you to marry me.'

'Well,' she laughed, 'I must say that every girl hopes a proposal will come from the man she loves, rather than the other way round. So how about it?'

He nuzzled close to her, his lips brushing against her cheek. 'April, my darling, will you marry me?'

'Hmm . . .' She giggled impishly. 'There's just one slight problem . . .'

'Oh, yes? And what would that be?'

'Finn. How on earth are we to tell him we're going to be married? I just won't be able to stand the look on his face!'

Emile Jacquot threw back his head and laughed from sheer joy. 'Then I'll tell him! *I'll* tell him!'
tell him!'

A Harlequin

ROBERTA LEIGH

Collector's Edition

A specially designed collection of six exciting love stories by one of the world's favorite romance writers—Roberta Leigh, author of more than 60 bestselling novels!

1 **Love in Store**
2 **Night of Love**
3 **Flower of the Desert**
4 **The Savage Aristocrat**
5 **The Facts of Love**
6 **Too Young to Love**

Available now wherever paperback books are sold, or available through Harlequin Reader Service. Simply complete and mail the coupon below.

Harlequin Reader Service

In the U.S.
P.O. Box 52040
Phoenix, AZ 85072-9988

In Canada
649 Ontario Street
Stratford, Ontario N5A 6W2

Please send me the following editions of the Harlequin Roberta Leigh Collector's Editions. I am enclosing my check or money order for $1.95 for each copy ordered, plus 75¢ to cover postage and handling.

☐ 1   ☐ 2   ☐ 3   ☐ 4   ☐ 5   ☐ 6

Number of books checked_____ @ $1.95 each = $_____

N.Y. state and Ariz. residents add appropriate sales tax $_____

Postage and handling $_____.75_____

TOTAL $_____

I enclose_____

(Please send check or money order. We cannot be responsible for cash sent through the mail.) Price subject to change without notice.

NAME_____
(Please Print)
ADDRESS_____ APT. NO._____

CITY_____

STATE/PROV._____ ZIP/POSTAL CODE_____

Offer expires February 29, 1984   30856000000